Clay tri

"I should have kno_
this." He clenched hi_
tempted to shake her.

"What are you doing here? I do not recall anyone inviting you." Nicola was surprised when her resentment at his appearance turned to a sudden pleasure at seeing him.

"Come, come, let us go to the office across the hall." Lord Willforde looked at the four men and Miss Nicola. "We have grave business to discuss."

Nicola followed the men and Willforde into a tiny office. The room was small but managed to hold six people. She tried to stand near the window but was forced, by the confines of the room, to stand directly in front of Mr. Barber.

She stood so close she could feel his breath from her head to her toes, as it caressed her body. A flame began a slow burn in her center. The longer they stood together the more liquid her knees became.

"I am Clay Barber. I have met Miss Nicola, but not you, sir." He inched past her toward Lord Willforde and shook hands.

She tried to shift her body but was forced to lean against the inside wall, in an attempt to bring her body temperature down and stay composed.

Praise for Z. Minor

"Wonderful story, great characters. A must read."
~Kathy Pritchett, author

The Sisterhood of the Coin

by

Z. Minor

The Sisterhood of the Coin

COPYRIGHT © 2015 by Louise Z. Pelzl

Cover Art by *Debbie Taylor*

The Wild Rose Press, Inc.
PO Box 708
Adams Basin, NY 14410-0708
Visit us at www.thewildrosepress.com

Publishing History
First Tea Rose Edition, 2015
Print ISBN 978-1-5092-0417-5
Digital ISBN 978-1-5092-0418-2

Published in the United States of America

Dedication

John—Thanks for believing in me.

Chapter One

London, England, January 24, 1820

Throughout the tedious journey, Nicola Highbridge gritted her teeth. Her body swayed as the mail coach collided with every hole and bump in the road. She discovered fighting the rocking movement of the vehicle made it harder to maintain her position on the carriage seat. At the last stop, Nicola secured a place next to a window, anchored herself in place by holding onto the edge of the black leather padded bench and planting her feet on the wooden carriage floor. Her right hand sought the ancient Roman coin deep in her traveling pocket throughout the trip. The uneasiness she felt with every breath increased her apprehension.

The open window let in enough fresh air to help mask the smells of body odor from the other passengers and the food they carried with them. The clickety-clack of the wheels moving across London's cobblestones announced they had reached their destination.

Eel, her young traveling companion, slipped out of the coach moments before the carriage ground to a stop. Cold, damp air rushed in. The door swung shut behind him.

The mail coach guard declared, as he positioned the steps. "Welcome to London, ladies and gents."

The gentleman closest to the exit tipped his hat to

the ladies in the carriage and leaped out, followed by his young son.

Eel stuck his head in the opening. "Miss, I 'elp you down."

Nicola slid across the cracked leather seat, pulling her herbal healing carryall along the carriage floor. She took the boy's hand, thankful to have solid ground under her feet, then removed her bag and sat it next to her on the dusty ground. She helped the last person, an elderly lady, down the unstable steps of the coach.

"Missy, here be your bags," shouted the driver, in a gruff voice, standing on top of the coach.

Two enormous cloth satchels soared through the air landing at her feet with a thud. Road dust danced around her. Nicola sneezed.

"Eel, which way do—"

Hearing no response, Nicola scanned the crowd milling around the mail coach. She located Eel standing next to a tall, hatless man. His hand coiled around the boy's arm. Nicola found it impossible to gain their attention. She left her luggage and side-stepped toward them.

"Where have you been hiding the past five days, my young friend?" she heard the man say, as he spun Eel around to face him.

Eel tried to take a step backward, but the man held on to his arm.

"I paid you! To assist me! Did you forget? I could—"

"I be explaining, sir. First, I must take the lady to her family's 'ome."

The man positioned his leg next to Eel's foot preventing the boy from moving in any direction.

2

"Sir, sir." Nicola brushed his coat sleeve with her hand to attract his attention.

He frowned at her. His clothes appeared to be those of a common laborer. Yet, they were perfectly tailored. His boots had been polished to a high gloss. His clean, red hair brushed and curled around the collar of his spotless, starched white shirt. He released Eel's arm and tightened his hand into a fist. His frown deepened. Obviously he didn't welcome her intrusion. However, this wasn't the first time she'd dealt with a man lacking in manners. Nor was it the first time her mind had grown too tired to think.

"Eel accompanied me to London from my home," she said, in a firm, strong voice. "It was a big responsibility for a young lad."

Nicola pulled her cape more securely about her shoulders. The man's imaginary touch journeyed first to her face, paused and then penetrated each layer of her clothing before it moved downward. The moment he looked away, the pulsing heat and panic vanished, leaving her cold.

"Oh bloody hell!"

Why do men have to swear? It is so unnecessary and shows their lack of vocabulary. Perhaps he is, after all, nothing more than a common laborer with new clothing.

"I beg your pardon, miss. I employed the boy more than two weeks ago. He and I have an agreement." He groaned, closed his eyes, shook his head, and then looked in her direction. "My name is Clay Barber. It will be an honor to escort you to your family's home. It is not safe for you to be walking the streets of London with only a lad for your protection—not even one as resourceful as Eel." He paused. "You, you do have a name?"

Nicola hesitated. She straightened her back and wet her lips. "It is Miss Nicola Highbridge. I thank you for your offer of assistance, but it is unwarranted." She took Eel's hand. "We are quite capable of reaching our destination without your guidance."

Why is this man trying to impose himself on me and treat me like a helpless goosecap? Does he think we cannot walk a few blocks in the daylight? I am a grown woman, quite competent to take care of myself. After all, I have been doing that for many years. He is making me cross as crabs.

Despite her protest, Mr. Barber walked to her bags and picked them up with little effort.

"Sir, it is unnecessary. Eel and I can manage."

"That may be. However, I will accompany you."

The boy tugged on her sleeve. "We be safe with 'im, miss."

Eel led the way. They marched single file down a narrow brick lane, onto yet another cobblestone street. Every uneven stone thrust through the thin soles of her new, fashionable boots purchased for the trip. She might live in a small backward town, but she didn't have to look like it.

The smell of rotting animal flesh wafted up around her and changed as she progressed down the street. The fetid and rancid smell of a privy, more than one she was sure, hung in the air. Decay and body odor intermingled with smoke from numerous fireplaces. Her eyes watered, and her throat grew dry. Even her hands felt dirty as air filtered through the gloves she wore. Trying to take deep breaths inched her stomach contents upward into her throat. Swallowing hard, she clamped her mouth shut and inhaled with small breaths through her nose, while she exhaled with her lips parted. Inwardly, she talked to her stomach until it calmed down and its contents stayed in place. Her teary eyes continued to itch. Using her lacy handkerchief, she dabbed at them as she walked. Carriages rumbled past, carts stacked with wooden boxes rushed around them, people of every shape and size made her forget her sore feet, and her hunger.

"I will not be ill, I will not be ill," she chanted, almost in a whisper, so no one could hear her.

Nothing would be more horrid than to cast up one's account in front of Mr. Barber. She wished she could walk behind him.

They traveled down two thoroughfares where the amount of traffic forced the carts, wagons, and coaches to drive slowly and with great caution. The trio dashed across the road, between the sluggish vehicles, to a narrow side street on the left, which was void of any traffic. Walking down two more quiet residential lanes, they reached a black iron gate in the middle of a tall, red brick wall. Not waiting for the others, Eel bounded through the opening and ran to the porch of the three story house. He scampered up the front stairs and grasped the brass doorknocker to announce their arrival.

Emmy opened the door and ran past Eel. "I knew you would come," she cried out and flung her arms around Nicola and whispered. "I'm so very glad you have arrived." Emmy raised her eyebrows at the man standing on the steps and directed him into the foyer. "Please carry the bags in." She pointed to the wall beneath the old painting of the English countryside.

"Set them there." Emmy turned to look at Nicola. "As usual, you are in time for tea."

"Emmy, I would like you to meet Eel's friend, Mr. Barber." Nicola hung her coat over the banister. She caught the smell of fresh mint mixed with rosemary and found a pot of fresh harvested herbs sitting on the plant stand next to the stairs. A deep breath brought back memories of the simple country cottage she had left behind. "Mr. Barber, this is my youngest sister, Miss Emmy Highbridge."

"I will wait for Eel outside." He bowed, touched his fingertips to his forehead, and walked out the door.

"When you are finished, Nicola, please join us for tea in the sitting room"—Emmy pointed—"through the door at the end of the hallway and then turn right. I do not think you have ever been to Aunt Belle's new estate." She turned back to Nicola. "We will talk later, Sister Dear."

My heart's desire, at this moment, would be to push or pull Emmy into a room, any room, and ask why she sent her coin.

Nicola sighed, knowing she would have to deal with her sister later. She turned and strolled toward Eel, who was now standing next to the front door.

"Eel, before you take your leave. I have a question for you. Would you be interested in being in my employment?"

"I be—"

The smile on the boy's face gave her the answer. Still she was relieved when he said, "Yes, miss. I be pleased to"—he paused for a moment, stood straighter and puffed out his chest—"to be in your service."

"Splendid. Can you come at ten in the morning?

We will discuss your duties." Nicola touched Eel's shoulder.

"Fine with me, miss."

She removed a coin from her pocket. "Here are your first wages. I felt very safe traveling with you, even in London."

Eel took the coin and hurried from the house. Nicola stood and enjoyed the cool movement of the air, as she watched the lad jump down the steps, and run down the sidewalk to meet Mr. Barber. She shut the door and entered the sitting room. It was green everywhere she looked—curtains, rugs, chairs, and seat covers. Every shade imaginable was represented. It must be Aunt Belle's new favorite color.

I do have some of the most peculiar relatives.

Nicola sat in the chair next to Aunt Belle and watched with amusement as her eccentric aunt poured from an ancient teapot Queen Elizabeth had given Aunt Belle's great-great-great-grandmother Alice, in 1562. The tea set covered the entire table top. Her foster sisters, Emmy and Mara sat directly across from Nicola and Aunt Belle. The poppy seed cakes and the hot, very hot tea would be refreshing and exactly what she needed after a tiring journey.

It would take Aunt Belle ages to finish telling them about her favorite subject—the Duke and Duchess of Kent, and their infant daughter, Victoria, who one day might be Queen of England.

Nicola yawned and waited for the chance to interrupt. "I am so tired. One would think sitting and doing nothing for hours would not have worn me out." She took Emmy's hand and pulled her up from her chair. "Please excuse us. Emmy will help me unpack, then I plan to retire for the evening. I cannot seem to keep my eyes open any longer. I look forward to seeing you all in the morning."

The moment Nicola shut the door behind them. Emmy whispered, "I am so glad you are here. I am—"

"Wait until we are in my room." Nicola touched Emmy's arm to get her attention. "You, my dear, have much to explain, but not where anyone can overhear us."

Nicola followed Emmy up the grand stairs leading to the second floor. The absence of voices vying for Nicola's attention gave her mind a much needed rest.

"Your room." Emmy stopped in front of the third door on the right. With a sweep of her hand she stood back to let Nicola enter. "It has a grand view of the new gardens Aunt Belle designed, and I must say she did a bang up job. They were completed last month."

"Why did Aunt Belle move? I remember she lived in a very fashionable estate, with a curved entrance. It was quite grand," Nicola said.

"Once dear Uncle William died, the house became too large and held too many memories. The *Ton* has taken no notice of Aunt Belle since Mara and I came to live here. Our lack of parentage and family history made her house off limits. A few old and dear friends still come to visit her from time to time. They and Aunt Belle don't give a darn about the *Ton* and their petty rules any more than Mara and I do."

Nicola walked into her room, which was bathed in soft candle glow and the flicker of flames in the fireplace. Emmy shut the door behind them, leaned against it, and began to sob. Nicola hurried back and gathered her distraught sister into her arms. Once the sudden outburst of tears passed, Nicola took Emmy by the hand. "Come now," she whispered. "I am here to help you. We must talk about this now!"

Nicola pried her sister's clasped hands apart, reached into her dress pocket, and removed a Roman coin which she placed in Emmy's palm. "Come, let us sit." She pushed her toward the fireplace.

"I did wonder if you would remember which coin belonged to me." Emmy continued to stand, as she turned the coin over and over in her hand. She set it on the side table.

"Yours is the huntress, mine the lion, and Mara's the chariot," Nicola said, recalling in detail each coin. "You could have sent a letter or at least a note explaining why I had to travel to London."

"I did not know where to start. It was easier to send the coin. I knew I could count on you," Emmy said, "and you would come at once."

Nicola put an arm around her sister and guided her to the chaise lounge next to the fireplace. "Sitting here will keep us warm."

"I have made an effort to be calm," Emmy said. "I-I am so thankful and relieved you are here." She hugged herself, rocking back and forth while looking at the floor.

"I am here to help." Nicola reached out and took Emmy's cold, shaking hands. "There is not anything we cannot accomplish together. Pray why have you sent for me?"

"I do not know where to start." Emmy chewed her lower lip. "George, he told me if I did not help him or told anyone, harm would come to Mara and Aunt Belle."

Emmy never could come right out and say what was amiss. Nicola struggled to stay composed. "You have me confused. Start at the beginning."

Emmy stared at the fire while she continued to bite her lip, eyebrows wrinkled to a frown. At some point in time, she would figure out where to start.

Nicola didn't have the patience to wait, not tonight. "Who is George? Does he have a surname?" She jumped up and paced around the room. Sitting still was hard for her at the best of times. Now she was afraid if she sat too long she might fall asleep, regardless of Emmy's predicament.

"The name I hear him called is George," said Emmy. "He works sometimes at the museum, unloading crates and moving artifacts from place to place. I have been organizing and arranging a new display." Emmy rubbed her hands together; her eyes twinkled with excitement. "Roman and Celtic treasures have been found in Culworth. Exceptional pieces, they are—"

"Stop. You can tell me about your wonderful exhibits later."

"Oh, my mind always wanders to my ancient relics. You know I do like to chatter about them." Emmy's shoulders sagged as she leaned back. "Sorry. Yes, well…about three weeks ago George came and told me he and his friends required my assistance." She tried to hide the tears gathering in her eyes by wiping them away with the back of her hand. "I was flattered until I realized they *demanded* my assistance. They have been stealing priceless objects. Stealing, can you imagine?" She continued to dab at her eyes with her handkerchief and then blew her nose.

"What was your role in their plan?" Nicola prodded her to continue.

"I am not quite sure. Many of the most valuable objects are locked up right and tight in a huge safe. I expect he thought I would hand over the priceless artifacts, without any questions." She stopped to take a breath. "I told them I could not, would not, and then he…" Emmy shut her eyes.

"You need to tell me the rest-now!" Nicola reached over, patted Emmy's hands, and sat down once more beside her.

"George said injury or death could come to my family." Emmy moaned. "I did not know what to do. Until I remembered my coin. You are the smartest and bravest of us, Sister Dear. I sent Eel to fetch you." She again paused and worried her lip. "In truth it was Mara's idea. She made me send Eel."

"And have you helped George and his friends?" Nicola held her breath.

Emmy shook her head. "I have not returned to the museum since George threatened me. Nor have I left the house. I did see George outside one morning." Emmy twisted her handkerchief into knots. "I sent a message to Lord Woodforde, the curator, telling him I was ill." She wrapped her arms around herself.

Nicola picked up a shawl from the foot of the bed and draped it across Emmy's shoulders.

"I am so very frightened for everyone in this house, and that now includes you. No one is safe," Emmy whispered.

"When do you have to return to the museum?"

"Today is, let me see"—Emmy glanced up at the ceiling—"is Monday. The display I am constructing is to open on March 23rd. I must dispatch a note telling the curator I will be back on February 1st which is one week from today."

"We will talk more in the morning and form a plan of action," Nicola said. "I have employed Eel. He and I can deliver a message to the museum for you, while we are out and about tomorrow."

"I am so thankful. You are a wonderful sister to have come." Emmy hugged her. "I feel safe, and I know you will be able to help me. Thank you, Sister Dear." Emmy handed her the shawl as she opened the door.

"We will talk in the morning."

Rummaging in the large dresser, Nicola couldn't find her nightgown and robe until she looked on the back of the green dressing screen. Her night apparel was hung on one of the wooden, carved pegs, designed to hold an assortment of garments. She also found her sweater and shawl. Nicola threw her clothes over the screen. She would hang them up in the morning.

Emmy's last words filtered back into her thoughts, but for some reason they seemed to revolve around the words, Sister Dear. Her brain was too tired to think any more. There was always tomorrow, and for a few seconds, she wondered what the day would bring.

Chapter Two

Clay Barber sat in the library smoking a cigar. There was little furniture in the rented house, other than the beds upstairs and a table in the kitchen, an old rickety office desk, two chairs, and a small table. The bookshelves lining the library walls were bare except for dust and cobwebs. The room smelled musty, damp even with the fireplace ablaze. The warmth didn't reach far into the room. Everything was covered in a layer of dust. The wind continued to rattle the dirty and smudged windowpanes, and on occasion a sudden draft rushed in from who knew where. He moved his chair closer to the fire and stretched out his legs. His conversation with Eel played through his mind. The boy had more nerve than sense.

"Mr. Barber, we—"

"Wait. *We*? If I wanted all of London to know I am looking for George"—Clay crossed his arms—"I would have put an advertisement in *The Times.*"

"Sir, me friends, Jeb and Jimmy, gave their word, they did. They be keeping it." Eel stared down at the floor, then at Clay. "Besides, they don't know about you. Not even your name. I told 'em, I be looking for me dear Uncle George."

It is easy to forget Eel is just a lad. I should not expect too much from one so young. Yet, somehow the boy and his friends have discovered George's last name, where he lives, and the fact he will be out of town until Monday. These three young lads provided me with more information than I could garner on my own. A job well done.

He gave Eel three coins, one for each boy, with a promise of more, beginning first thing on Monday morning.

Clay still could not believe that countrywoman had hired Eel, right under his very nose. She did it to put him in a pickle. Miss Highbridge was starting to occupy his thoughts and to interfere in his carefully laid plans.

Damn, what a nuisance that woman is! This could really put me in a coil, if I'm not careful. I need to put a stop to this nonsense immediately.

****

At daybreak Clay shaved and dressed, while he structured his strategy down to the very last detail. Leaving by the back door kept him from having to talk to any of his neighbors. He found it hard to remember the lies he would have to tell to explain his presence in this run-down part of town. It was easier and safer for all concerned to remain anonymous.

He stayed in the shadows, as he approached the Highbridges' family home. The house was dark except for one window where a light shone. Clay believed it was the kitchen. He knocked twice. A scullery maid opened the door, and a sliver of light sneaked through the crack.

"What you want?" she squeaked.

"I must see Miss Highbridge, Miss Nicola Highbridge. It is urgent."

The door shut in his face, but he could hear muffled voices. He leaned against the doorframe, and when he lifted his arm to knock again, the door sprang open. An older woman stood in the entrance. A huge white apron dusted with flour covered her oversized body.

"Miss Highbridge will be seeing you." She motioned with her spoon for him to enter.

The fresh baked bread made his mouth water. The sizzling bacon prompted his stomach to growl. The smell of the working kitchen reminded him of his ancestral home—the wonderful meals served there, his parents whom he missed, and his murdered brother.

Handing him a piece of bacon, the cook motioned him to follow the housemaid. He wanted to eat the meat as slowly as possible, to savor the smoky flavor, but his hunger won out. Two bites, and it was gone.

A few minutes later, he was led into a massive library; shelves and shelves of books of all shapes and sizes covered every space. Books cascaded around every one of the chairs in the room. He picked up one of the tomes, *Culpeper's Complete Herbal* as Nicola walked in.

"Good morning, Mr. Barber. I see I am not the only person up and about at this time of the morning." She sat in the chair nearest the fire. "Tea will arrive in a few minutes, along with some baked goods."

He gave her the book, walked over to the fire, and stretched his fingers toward the warmth. In his haste he'd forgotten his gloves. He rubbed his hands together, hoping to rush the heat not only to his hands but his entire body.

When the tea service arrived, she invited him, with a flick of her hand, to sit in the chair across the table from her. They sipped their tea and devoured the baked scones, hot from the oven and dripping with honey, before he wiped his lips and said.

"I am sure you are wondering why I called on you, without an invitation."

"I am sure you are about to tell me."

"I have come about Eel. You have to understand, he agreed to assist me long before you were known to him." He placed the cup and saucer on the table. "It is important he be available when I require his services." He rose and walked back to the fireplace. He didn't want her to see his body's sudden reaction to her.

"He is just a lad. How much can a little boy assist you, I wonder?"

"You do not understand our young lad, do you?" Not waiting nor expecting a response, he continued. "Eel is not any street lad. He is the most liked and respected urchin in all of London. He seems to know everyone and I mean everyone."

Londoners, Clay discovered when he first arrived, offered more information if they thought they were aiding one of their own, and Eel was a true Londoner.

"What type of tasks do you require of him?" Nicola asked.

If I tell her who I am and what I am doing, she will bandy it about. I don't expect her to be any different from other women I have met.

"I am not at liberty to discuss his tasks, as you call them."

"Well, if you will not tell me anything…"

Rubbing his jaw to keep his temper from showing on his face, he tried to reason. "He is helping me find—" He started to cough to cover the man's name he almost revealed. He could not believe her intriguing charm, and his befuddled mind where she was concerned had almost been his undoing.

"Eel and I have yet to discuss his duties," she said. "But I will take your request into consideration." She took the book from her lap and placed it on the floor with the others. "I am sure we can work out a schedule of sorts, which will meet with your approval. However, I request you do the same for me."

"I cannot make any promises," he said.

"Then neither can I." She stood. "I will escort you to the door."

Walking down the stairs onto the sidewalk, he marched to the iron gate, and turned back to look at the house.

That woman is more than I can abide. First she twists around my words, and then acts like she owns the boy. Well, my mission for the government comes first.

****

Her wool shawl settled around her shoulders, Nicola rambled through the downstairs rooms, waiting for Eel. Once the upstairs maid handed her the message from Emmy, Nicola marched back into the library, throwing the shawl on top of the books on the floor. She couldn't believe the note she held in her hand.

Sister Dear,

I am so relieved you have arrived. I have gone to Culworth to dig for Roman artifacts. I expect to return late Sunday eve. I know you will have the solution to our problem upon my return.

Your loving sister,

Emmy

P.S. Please deliver the second note to Lord Woodforde at the museum.

17

Her anger at Emmy for leaving to go and unearth her ancient treasures was beyond the pale. Mr. Barber's morning visit had distracted her, allowing Emmy to sneak out of the house while she was occupied.

Sister Dear indeed. This is Emmy's way of trying to get someone else, me, to take over her responsibilities. Well, not this time.

Nicola stemmed her outburst and glanced around the room to reserve her criticisms for its decor. Why would anyone, even Aunt Belle, want an entire house decorated in hues of the same color? Some of the shades were disgusting: pea soup was not the color for chair coverings, nor that solid dark green for curtains. Made one feel like being in a forest, a never-ending one. Any minute birds would start to sing and deer would bound through the room. Cheered by her flights of fancy and happy only she was aware of them, she brought herself back to reality.

In the sitting room, she subsided into yet another green chair. At least sitting in this one, Nicola didn't feel like she was on top of a slimy, green, water pond.

Maybe, if she sat still for a time she could understand all the hubble-bubble going on around her.

Why ever did I hire Eel? Was it to anger Mr. Barber? Smiling to herself, she ignored the possible answers. It would be best to have Eel acquaint her with London.

As if on cue, footsteps sounded in the hallway. Nicola walked to the doorway. "Good morning, Eel." She beckoned him into the room. "I have a question."

Eel moved inside the door with his hat in his hand.

"What is your Christian name?"

"Me what name?"

"Do you have a name other than Eel?"

He glanced at the floor, as he moved closer to her. He motioned her to bend down to him and whispered in her ear.

"Even me mom don't use that there name," he said, standing tall.

Nicola sat in the chair closest to the fireplace. Even with a roaring fire, the room was cold and damp. She gathered her shawl off the books and wrapped it around her shoulders, before turning to Eel, sitting in the chair next to her.

"I like the name Eli, but will call you Eel if you insist."

"Please miss."

"Eel it is," she said. "We will determine your duties as we move through the days ahead. I will pay you an honest wage." An idea popped into her head. "Might you have an interest in learning to read and write?"

His eyes grew wide.

"If you are going to be in my service, you will need to be able to do both. I believe I can teach you. In my day, I was a fair student."

Nicola failed to mention that the tutors hired by her foster mother, over the years praised her as one of the best students they had the pleasure of teaching. One had been sacked because he commented that her brilliant mind was wasted on a mere girl.

"Oh, miss, Miss Nicola. I be—I wants to speak proper—like a gentleman. I be working for nothin'—'ffing I could learn." He stopped to catch his breath. "Oh, first you needs to meet me mum. That be, before I be allowed to accept your em—" He cleared his throat.

"Employment."

"It will be an honor to meet your mother. I could explain about your duties and your lessons. Do you think I could see her this afternoon?"

"I be thinking. Now be best. I mean…" His hat moved from hand to hand.

She smiled at his enthusiasm and her own, her earlier upset vanished. An education would be the opportunity for Eel to improve his station in life.

"Let me get my cape and reticule." She stood and smoothed the wrinkles from her dress and dropped her shawl on the chair. "Can we walk, or do I need to hire a carriage?"

"We can be walking. My mom ain't far, miss."

Nicola touched Eel's shoulder. "Your first lesson: the proper words are 'is not' not 'ain't'." She listened and nodded her approval when he said the words correctly.

The sun broke through the clouds. Damp, musty air and the smell of burning coal greeted them as they walked down the street. Breathing into her handkerchief, doused with herbal oils, helped cover the odors of the city.

Not far from home, a small child tumbled down three stairs. Nicola ran to her.

"Oh dear, what have you done to yourself?"

The child, a girl about six or seven years of age, began to cry. A group of children formed a circle around them.

"Lizzie, the lady be talkin' to you." Eel looked down at the child. "You best answer 'er."

"I fall down, I did." Pulling out her leg, she pointed to blood seeping around the newest tear in her well-mended stocking.

"Well, Lizzie, I have just the remedy." Reaching into her reticule, Nicola removed a small corked bottle, and a clean handkerchief edged with lace. She poured lavender oil on the cut to prevent infection. After securing the makeshift bandage around Lizzie's leg, Nicola helped the child to her feet.

Whispering into Lizzie's ear, Eel nudged her toward Nicola.

"Oh, thank you, miss. Me 'urt feels eber so much better."

"You will need to replace your stockings." Nicola produced a coin, which she gave to Lizzie. "Now, off you go and do be careful."

"Oh, thank you, miss." The little girl closed her hand around the coin as she curtsied. "And your—" Lizzie pointed to Nicola's handkerchief.

Nicola touched the girl's hand. "You may keep it."

Eel and Nicola continued down the street crowded with the working class. Wagons and carts were busy making deliveries and blocking traffic. She was intrigued with the hustle and bustle of people running here and there, like a bunch of ants.

"Good morning, sir." Nicola nodded her head in a man's direction. "How are you today, madam?" She smiled at a woman passing by. "Might I help?" Nicola took one handle of a heavy clothes basket and walked two blocks with a washerwoman. "Eel, why is everyone looking at me as if I have grown two heads?"

"You, miss. No one be used to seeing a lady acting so nice to 'em."

"I still do not understand. Back home everyone helped everyone—no matter their station. To assist women was expected. The—" A man pushed aside a woman carrying a large awkward tub. "Oh, I see." She stopped and thought about Mr. Barber carrying her bags to Aunt Belle's house.

Running back, Eel slid to a stop in front of her. "Somethin' wrong miss?"

Nicola shook her head. "Simply stopped to think."

Eel and his mother lived in a loft above Creations, a dress shop, owned by her foster sister Mara. Eel's mother was head seamstress and managed the shop. Taking a key from around his neck, Eel opened the back door. The moment they walked up the back stairs, loud, angry voices could be heard.

"That there be me mum and a..." Eel grabbed her arm. "I not be understanding the words."

I think they are speaking..." Putting two fingers to her lips she said, "Ssshhh. They are speaking Welsh, I believe. Come with me." When Eel hesitated, she pulled him out the door, down the stairs, and around to the front of the shop. "Do not say anything. Follow my lead."

The hard set of his jaw suggested Eel might not listen to her.

"It will be fine, trust me." Nicola opened the shop's front door.

Their arrival, announced by a small bell, was not heard over the din of the shouting.

"Hello, is anyone here?" Nicola called out.

A woman hurried to the main sales floor from a side room. Drawn lips emphasized her angry, red cheeks, and her deepening frown.

"Yes, madam?"

A man marched up behind the woman. His long

strides carried him past her to the front entrance in seconds.

"I will be back," he barked. "You can count on it." The man opened the door and then slammed it.

The room was silent except for the vibration of the windowpane, which hummed and quivered in the doorframe.

Eel ran to his mother. "The man did not 'urt you, did 'e?"

"No. He is just angry, child." The look on his mother's face softened as she gathered the boy in her arms and hugged him.

Nicola cleared her throat. "Excuse me, I am Nicola Highbridge and have come to discuss Eel's employment. However, if today is inconvenient. I could return at another time.

Eel's mother put her hand on her son's shoulder. "I be Susan Summers and now appears to be a fine time. With the sun shining, our customers, unless I miss my guess, would rather be out and about enjoying the splendid weather than being in a stuffy dress shop."

Nicola outlined what she believed would be Eel's duties and his schooling.

"How can I ever thank you?' asked Susan.

"It is my pleasure to help such a wonderful lad. I believe we will be helping each other. Thank you for letting him be my guiding light while I am in London."

After a tour of Creations, Nicola felt it necessary to hire a hackney to take them to the museum to deliver Emmy's note to the curator. The man in the shop reminded her there were unsavory characters in a city like London. After all, it wasn't like back home where she knew everyone.

Chapter Three

Nicola and Eel struggled to open the museum's ancient wooden door. The only piece of furniture, in the cavernous entrance was an old, blackened table. A man appeared and pointed to a small sign, sitting in the center of the table, "Information Desk."

"We are here to see Lord Woodforde," Nicola stated.

The man moved closer. His jacket, too large for his slender build, hid his hands from view. His frail features and raised eyebrows reminded her of a country scarecrow without the straw padding. An odor of stale and rancid cooked fish hung in the air. Perched on the very tip of his long, pointed nose were small round glasses. Tilting his head back to peer through the lenses, he somehow managed to keep them balanced in place. His Adam's apple looked like a goose egg sliding up and down his throat.

"Do you have an appointment, miss?" asked the man, in a toplofty voice.

"We do not. However, I have a message from my sister, Miss Emmy Highbridge. It is my understanding Lord Woodforde has been waiting to hear from her."

"You may leave the message with me." He extended his hand. A long pause followed, before he placed his arm behind his back and lowered his chin.

"I think not. We can wait or return at a later time."

"At this very moment, he is in a meeting, which might last a good hour or more." The man leaned toward them. "If you must wait"—the man sighed—"you can browse through the museum. I will notify Lord Woodforde you are here." He glanced down at the tabletop and began shuffling papers from one stack to another.

"Thank you, we will do that Mr…?"

"Pagger. Mr. Pagger, Miss…"

"Miss Nicola Highbridge and Mr. Eli Summers," Nicola replied.

Eel nodded his head toward the man.

Turning, Nicola took the boy's hand and walked away.

"Sorry about the name," she whispered. "I could not introduce you as Eel. It would not do, not to Mr. Pagger." She pointed her chin in the air.

Eel giggled.

They strolled into the first room and found row after row of glass cases. A map of the entire museum was printed on the far wall, along with a directory of collections. The library contained the History of Heraldry.

Nicola retraced her steps to tell Mr. Pagger where they could be found, but he was no longer standing guard. She took a sheet of paper from the stack on the corner of the table, picked up a pen, dipped it into the open ink well, and scribbled a note.

Nicola and Eel stopped often to marvel at the tapestries, paintings, and drawings that hung on various walls. Nicola wrinkled her nose. The smells of dust, mildew, and decay hung in the air. They weren't unpleasant, but noticeable, and what one would expect to find in a museum.

The library was massive. Books stood in neat rows on shelves that reached floor to ceiling and lined every wall in the huge room. A maze of short bookcases filled the center and branched out over the floor. What secrets could the greatest library in all of London and England have hidden in these walls?

Could this be the place I should begin my search for my birth parents?

With nothing to do until Emmy returned from Culworth on Sunday, Nicola, rather than be idle for even a minute, decided to use her time to gather information about the people who gave her life. When Nicola was a mere two days old, her birth parents presented her to Catherine Highbridge, her wonderful foster mother, to raise. Nicola never understood why her parents gave her away like old clothing. For some strange and unexplained reason, they also left two gifts that were given to her on her eighteenth birthday. It didn't make any sense then and certainly not now.

One of the presents was a replica of a man's signet ring that she believed had belonged to her father. What better place to begin a search for the griffin on the ring than a library? Past studies of the animal proved it to be both popular and unique because no two were alike. One had to study each griffin to discover the differences, but they were there.

Nicola with little effort located the heraldry section by following the small signs, which were categories. She took the signet ring from her reticule and put it on her right ring finger so she could study it without fear of dropping it. The ring fit as if it had been made for her, which of course, was impossible.

"Miss, might I be seeing the ring?" Eel asked.

"First, the correct words are 'might I see,' not 'I be seeing'."

Taking off the ring, she placed it in Eel's outstretched hand.

"What kind of stone be this, miss?" The boy turned the ring this way and that.

"An emerald, which is an unusual choice for a signet ring."

"This is a special kind of ring?"

"Yes, it is also considered a privy seal. People use them to seal letters and important documents. Melted wax is dripped on the document or letter. Before the wax cools, the ring is pressed into the wax replicating the emblem in the wax."

"I think I be understanding," Eel said. "When the letter be opened the seal be broken. Do I have it right, miss?"

"Yes, you do. The broken seal also tells the intended receiver if anyone else has opened the letter or document. The seal identifies the sender because each signet ring is unique."

"Can anyone be havin' a ring?" Eel asked.

"I suppose, but in most cases peerage or gentry have them."

"What be peer-peerage?"

"Hum. Peerage is a title of nobility. Like a duke, earl, or even a king."

"What kind of animal be a griffin?" Eel handed the ring back. "I can't be seeing it very well."

"It is a fabulous beast. It has the body of a lion, the head and wings of an eagle. You might not be able to see it, but right below the bottom of this animal"—she pointed to the wreath at the base—"is a number seven."

"What does the seven mean, miss?"

"I do not know." She sighed. "This is one of the mysteries. This ring is small because it is made for a woman. A man's ring would be much larger, easier to see the details."

She examined the books and decided to look at the first one. Hoping to find some drawings or pictures, anything that would identify her griffin, she started to read.

"Good day. Might I assist you?"

She stared at a man who had appeared out of nowhere and was standing on the other side of the bookcase. She clamped her hand around the ring.

Eel appeared to have lost interest and wandered away, but Nicola saw him hurry back the moment the man started speaking.

"I am trying to find the origins of a griffin on a signet ring." She smiled while resting her arm along the top of the bookcase, her hand still closed around the ring. "I am hoping to find a book with drawings. Are we in the right section?"

"You are in the correct area." The man stepped closer. "I am well versed in heraldry and might be able to aid in your search if you can describe the crest in some detail."

"I can show you rather than explain," Nicola handed him the ring.

The man studied it. "You could leave it with me." He wet his upper lip with the tip of his tongue. "I could do a search for you."

"I cannot leave it." Nicola reached out for the ring.

The man placed it on the bookcase and pushed it in

her direction. She slipped it back on her finger. "However, thank you for your kind offer."

"Leave me information on how I may contact you. I will do some research. If I find anything of importance, I will let you know straight away."

Since she acquired the ring she had learned having it did not mean she could identify the owner. Nicola reached into her reticule for one of her calling cards. She had written Aunt Belle's address on the back of a few, after Mr. Barber left this morning.

Perhaps this man might be able to aid in my search.

"Miss Highbridge."

At the sound of her name, Nicola turned toward the door. A man, dressed in a suit and cravat, moved toward her.

"Lord Woodforde, at your service." He bowed his head as he took her hand in his. "I am sorry you have been waiting, but meetings you know? Someone is always calling one to discuss something. Between you and me, most meetings do not accomplish much, just a lot of chit-chat." He walked over to the open book. "While you were waiting, I hope you found something interesting to occupy your time."

"Yes, this nice gentleman…" Looking around the library, she found the man had disappeared, along with Eel. "Excuse me, Lord Woodforde," she said, hiding her confusion. "My reason for coming to the museum was to deliver this message from my sister, Miss Emmy Highbridge." Nicola removed the sealed note from her reticule and handed it to him.

"I hope Miss Highbridge has recovered from her illness and will return soon to finish the Celtic exhibit."

He opened the note with a flourish but didn't look at it. "Her excellent work on the museum artifacts is a very important part of our Heritage Display. The directors at the museum have great expectations for the exhibit. Of utmost importance is the hope to entice people to donate money to modernize our facilities. We have many treasures which cannot be shown due to the deteriorating condition of some of our buildings."

"Emmy is recovering and will be back on February 1st."

"Wonderful, wonderful." Lord Woodforde put the still unread note in his jacket pocket. "I will make sure her work area is arranged to her liking. May I invite you to partake of some refreshments?"

"No thank you, sir. We must be goin'." Eel said, moving to stand next to Nicola.

She stared at the lad. There was no mistaking his tone nor the look of conviction on his face. It was time to leave.

"Who are you, young man?" Lord Woodforde looked down at Eel.

"I be—"

"May I introduce my young friend?" Nicola interrupted. "Mr. Eli Summers."

Lord Woodforde and Eel shook hands.

"Thank you for your kind offer of tea. We must leave. A pleasure to meet you, sir." She smiled and offered her hand to the gentleman. "I look forward to seeing the Heritage Display."

The minute they got to the display case room, she stopped the boy with a gentle tug on his sleeve.

"Young man, what is wrong?"

"Watched the man go through them doors in the far

corner, I did. Figured somet'ing be wrong. 'E should have stayed. So I follows 'im. He met up with Mr. Pagger."

"Seems natural for them to meet after all they both work in the museum."

"I couldn't be hearing all they said, because them walked away from me 'iding place. I did 'ear 'em mention your ring."

"It did seem rather strange one minute he was there and the next he was gone," she replied, glancing around to make sure no one overheard them. "I thought perhaps he was not supposed to be in the library."

Nicola hastened as fast as she could without drawing attention to herself. She and Eel hurried to the front entrance. Mr. Pagger was not in sight. They managed to pull open the front door and hurried down the stairs. There were no hackneys in sight. Eel suggested they walk to Great Russell Street where a carriage could easily be found. The sun peeked out from behind the clouds, and the wind picked up momentum.

"I wonder why the man and Mr. Pagger are so interested in my ring."

"I might be knowing of someone who can 'elp us. I be asking 'im tonight."

"Thank you." She took Eel's hand. "The correct word is 'help' not ''elp'."

Chapter Four

By mid-morning Barnaby Roget, Clay's business partner, brought news of the Spenceans' latest campaign—a murderous plan against the government.

The conspirators were members of a group of Spencean Philanthropists, named after Thomas Spence, a British radical speaker. The group led by Arthur Thistlewood was angry over economic and political oppression. They planned to overthrow the government and oversee a radical revolution.

A hurried meeting of the King's Men (KM6), was called. These men never gathered in the same place or at the same time. A vacant office in a building across from the British Museum was ideal for their purposes. However, it proved to be cold, drafty, and smelled of rats and mice, and so they concluded their meeting in short order. The six men varied their departures. Clay and Barnaby stood at the corner debating which way to go. The wind whipped around the buildings, and once again Clay's hands were cold as he had forgotten his gloves.

Clay's former commander had offered him the opportunity, two months ago, to help the crown find and destroy the Spenceans' organization, but more importantly to find the men who financed and led them. He jumped at the chance. The assignment gave him a way to seek revenge for the death of his brother, which had been arranged by the Spenceans under disguise of a robbery gone wrong.

Clay hoped to lay his demons to rest. He wanted his life back. Maybe not the exact one, but one that was close to it would do. He once had been a carefree rake, a second son. Now he was the only son with duties, obligations, and responsibilities. He could never go back, but would he ever be able to move forward?

"Well, well, look who is leaving the museum," Clay pointed in the direction of the museum steps.

"Should I be surprised, you are talking about a woman? And by the looks of her, a rather attractive one." Barnaby laughed. "I thought you'd sworn off women, at least until our mission is complete."

Clay tried to ignore Nicola strolling down the street. But when a man scurried from the back of the museum and fell in behind her, and the lad, his mouth dropped open.

"Do you see what I see?" Barnaby asked.

"I do, but why would anyone, follow those two? We better join the parade to make sure the lady and the lad do not get into any trouble."

That woman is ruining my life. First my plans, then my morning, and now the rest of the day. Damn, I knew she was trouble the first time I saw her.

****

Eel learned early in life always to be alert to his surroundings. There were times London streets were not safe, even in the daylight hours. Within a block of the museum, he observed a man following them. When they stopped, the man did as well.

When Nicola lingered at the millinery store window in the center of the block, Eel dropped to the ground pretending to tie his shoelace. A large floppy hat hid the face of the man who came to an abrupt stop at the mercantile store on the corner. In frustration and worry, Eel jumped up. The street was deserted except for two familiar-looking men, their coats flapping behind them as they hurried along. At this point they were too far away to offer any assistance.

Nicola didn't appear to be in any hurry. If he was wrong, which could be possible, it was best not to worry her. He could protect Miss Nicola from the likes of a common thief.

"I see an apothecary shop," Nicola said. "I must go in and see if they have fresh herbs for sale."

"Now?" Eel asked.

"You may venture in with me."

"I be waiting 'ere."

"I will not be long, I promise. The word is 'here', not ''ere'."

Eel stood outside the building for a few seconds and darted into the mews hoping to double back to the two men, but he couldn't locate them. He dashed back to the front of the apothecary shop as Mr. Barber leaned his back against the window box on the corner.

"Mr. Barber, what you be doin'?"

Clay spun around to face Eel.

"So, you did see us. I hoped you had. This is Barnaby Roget, my closest friend. He is assisting me in the search for your dear Uncle George."

Eel faced Barnaby who was a few inches shorter and a little heavier than Mr. Barber. He had a scar across his left cheek, startling blue eyes, and dark, almost black, hair. Eel shook his extended callused hand.

"Pleased to be meeting you, Mr. Roget."

"Barnaby, lad, just Barnaby."

"Care to tell us why you and the lady are being followed."

Eel shook his head. "Not be knowing. We done delivered a message to the gent in charge for 'er sister, Miss Emmy. We 'ad to wait, so went lookin' at books, all shapes and sizes. Miss Nicola had a—"

"Why would someone have an interest in the two of you?" Clay turned back to watch the front of the shop.

"Eel, you best go inside," Barnaby said, as he slipped around the side of the building."

Clay poked his head around the corner. "I saw your new friend come out of the shop. You get the lady into the carriage that will be waiting at the door. We will entertain the follower for a time."

Without making a sound, Eel hastened to the shop door, entered, and walked up to Nicola. "We must leave now," he whispered. "Our carriage be waiting. I be explaining on our way 'ome."

"What carriage? We did not...I mean we do not have one. And the word is 'home' not ''ome'."

Eel raised his eyebrows as the follower walked back into the shop. All he could see was the back of the gent's covered head. Eel took Nicola's hand and gently tugged on her arm.

"Excuse me, Mr. Random; it appears we are leaving. I will be back in the next few days to order more supplies. Please send me the items we discussed. Here is my address." Nicola handed him one of Aunt Belle's calling cards. She had already signed and paid for her order.

She was relieved she'd taken off her gloves because somehow ink had gotten on her hand. Removing her handkerchief from her reticule, she wiped at the spot to make sure the ink was dry before putting her gloves on as the day had turned misty and cold.

"Excellent, Miss Highbridge, I look forward to serving you. Your purchases will be delivered tomorrow morning as the deliveryman has already left today with the afternoon orders."

Eel helped Nicola into the waiting carriage, jumped in, and squeezed next to the door, forcing her to sit away from the window. Nicola glowered at Eel as the carriage pulled away.

"What has gotten into you today? You are—" She frowned at Eel. "Young man, I hope you have a good explanation for making me leave and acting so peculiarly. I had not finished. And I do not like being ordered about."

"Yes miss, I got good reason." He let the curtain fall back into place as the carriage merged into traffic. "Someone from the museum followed us."

"Wait, someone was, is, following us. But you don't know who or why?"

Eel nodded his head. "Mr. Barber and Barnaby saw the gent too. They be going to stop him."

"None of this makes any sense. Who is Barnaby?"

Clay and Barnaby stood on each side of the shop door. The follower exited, and each man seized an arm and propelled him into the mews at the far side of the building. An old fence propped up by a broken down wagon offered them protection from prying eyes.

"You—you put me down. Do you 'ear me? I ain't

got no money nor valuables." He screwed up his face as his voice squeaked. "You be not'ing but footpads."

The man tried to wrench his arms from the men's grip. He found he couldn't. He was six inches shorter and didn't have the strength against the two who towered over him. His head continued to rotate from side to side.

Barnaby whispered and talked very rapidly. "We don't want your valuables, just information." He removed the man's hat and threw it on the ground.

"Why are you following the lady and the young lad?" Clay growled and tightened his hold on the man's arm.

"Mr. Pagger. He told me to follow her and tell him where she went. Mind you, I were not to talk to her."

"Who is Mr. Pagger? You always do as he says?"

"He be me boss at the museum. If I want to keep me job, I do what Pagger says."

"What is your name?"

"I not be saying. Iffin' it be all the same to you."

"Your name?" Clay demanded. "I will not ask again."

The man sighed. "Jasper Arts."

"Well, it appears you have two options. You gather some information for us, or you go to Newgate. You best decide which it is to be." Clay released the man's arm.

"You know Newgate might not be bad," Barnaby said. "When a man ain't had a woman in a long time, some prisoners begin to think some of the newcomers might be able to take a woman's place. Iffin' you know what I mean?"

"I don't know who you be. I suppose you cannot be

any worse than working for Pagger, believe me."

"I am Clay Barber and he"—Clay pointed in his partner's direction—"is Barnaby Roget. All you have to do is find out why Pagger has an interest in the lady. When you do, go to the Hog's Head Inn and leave me a message."

"Do you think you can do that?" Barnaby asked.

"Do I have a choice?"

"No." Clay and Barnaby said in unison.

"Well?" Clay asked.

"I can be doing that."

"Then be gone with you. Remember we know where to find you," Clay said.

Barnaby pointed his finger at the man. "Do not play games with us." He leaned his hand on the hilt of his dagger, which dangled from his belt, and continued to stare at the man.

"What do I tell Pagger? Pray tell." The man looked at the knife in Barnaby's belt. Then out of the corner of his eye he glanced at Clay, then at Barnaby and then again at the knife.

"Tell him the lady got in a carriage on High Holborn, and you could not follow her." Clay slapped him on the back.

Both men watched as Jasper picked up his foot-trodden hat and hurried down the mews to the side road.

"What do you think will happen to him?" Barnaby asked.

"It all depends how well he can lie to Pagger. It is too bad. He seems honest enough, just working for the wrong person. I'll talk to someone and arrange a job for him out of the city."

Chapter Five

Nicola closed her eyes and pressed her head back against the squabs, trying to stop the whirling confusion in her mind. Mr. Barber's face suddenly clouded her vision. Her eyes opened in a flash. Yet the man remained in her thoughts and added to her baffled state of mind.

I should have stayed in quiet Chew Magna. My life might have been dull and most of the time uneventful, but I was in control.

Cold air followed Nicola into the house as she pushed open the front door. Her mind remained puzzled and confused. First the man disappeared from the library, and then someone followed them. Could there be a common thread? She entered the foyer and a cloak of protection fell over her while she stood in Aunt Belle's London house. Her small cottage in Chew Magna was all but forgotten, at least for a time.

"Miss, what be that awful sound?" Eel shut the outside door behind them.

Listening, she shook her head. "I—I do not know, but I suggest we discover the source."

They followed the howling into the kitchen. Betsy, the housemaid, hovered over the cook in near hysterics.

"Oh, my," Nicola said.

Betsy began to wail louder. Cook's right elbow was positioned on the kitchen table. Her forearm extended upward with her head propped on her right hand. She was blowing her breath, for all she was worth, on her burned left arm, which was suspended in the air a few inches above the table.

"Betsy, go to my room. Get my red bag. It is on the floor of the large wardrobe."

"Miss, I must stay with Cook. 'Er needs me."

"I will take good care of her. Now go and fetch the bag." Nicola whispered in Eel's ear. He left pulling Betsy along.

With a tender touch, Nicola placed her hand on Cook's shoulder. "I have come to offer my assistance. Please show me what you have done."

"Oh, miss. It be the cat." She rested her arm on the table and continued to blow on the burned area. "She ran between me legs, tangled up in my skirt. I put the beef roast in the oven. I fell forward, and me arm hit the corner of the hot oven door." Cook held up her arm, a long, angry, red, blistering burn started a few inches above her wrist and continued up the length of her forearm. "In no time I be fine."

The cat sauntered over to the table and rubbed up against Nicola's legs. She glared down at the animal, which was quick to run under the stove.

"You better hide. If I catch you…"

"Miss Nicola, do not mind the cat, she is a good mouser. After me arm stops burning a mite. I be putting some butter on it."

Nicola caught herself before she shouted and said in a normal tone. "You will not."

"But, miss—"

"Butter is not the remedy to use for a burn. We want to take the heat out. Butter seals the heat in. First, we pour cold water on your burn to cool it off. Then we will cover your blistered area with my healing salve. You'll see. It will be better by morning."

"I never heard of such a thing." Cook shook her head. "But I trusts you, miss."

Nicola placed an empty bucket on the floor. She put Cook's arm hand down into the bucket and poured cool water over the burned area. She emptied the bucket and continued to pour fresh, cool water over her arm. Nicola took a bottle of salve from her herbal bag and with great care smoothed some on the burn. Betsy and Eel watched Nicola's every move. Taking a rolled strip of white cloth from her bag, she was careful not to wrap the bandage around Cook's arm too tightly.

Nicola finished making dinner. The cook gave her detailed instructions and supervised her every move. During her cooking lesson, while she was looking for potatoes, Nicola discovered a storage room, a perfect place for her herbal studies, and the best and far most interesting feature: a door leading to the outside.

Would it be possible to establish a much needed herbal study area? Even if it was temporary? *I don't like to be idle. It would give me an opportunity to study people in a large city and compare their ills to those of people living in rural areas.*

Discovering she rather enjoyed cooking left no time to think about the museum, the follower, Mr. Barber, and his friend. Her thoughts were of dinner and the cook's blistered arm.

Watching in amusement, Nicola rather enjoyed Betsy and Eel licking the wooden spoons and using their fingers to get every drop of cake frosting off every utensil she used, including the bowl. Their antics entertained the entire kitchen staff.

Later in the evening, sitting in the library, Nicola recalled the follower, and the man at the museum. Her thoughts lasted a few minutes before she decided none of it made any sense.

It has been some kind of blunder on my part. That is the answer to all of this foolish intrigue. The entire episode isn't worth thinking about.

However, Mr. Barber was another matter. He appeared to be her knight in shining armor. First walking her to Aunt Belle's house because he thought London was dangerous and now protecting her from a follower. For a moment, her mind held a picture of being held in his arms on his trusty white steed. Nicola shook her head and pulled her shawl tighter around her shoulders.

****

The next morning, Nicola sat trying to be patient and quiet waiting for Eel. Her day was crammed with too much to do. Her right foot tapped the floor, until she jumped up and began to pace the room. Hearing the boy's approach, she walked toward the door.

"Good morning, miss." Eel strolled into the room.

"Yes, it is a wonderful morning. I am afraid it will prove to be a very busy one." She gestured to the chairs, and they sat down. "Each working day will begin with a meeting to discuss our plans." She took a plate of biscuits and offered him one. She'd already eaten two and would have eaten more but wanted to save some for Eel. "First, we must go back to the apothecary shop, then on to the bookshop for your books and supplies." She brought her cup to her mouth, took a sip, and grimaced as she put her cup on the table.

The tea was ice cold. "Later this afternoon, we will start to clean my herbal room." She stopped talking, sat still, and took a deep breath.

"What be an herbal room, miss?" Eel brushed crumbs from his trousers into his hand, and placed them onto his napkin.

"Come, I will show you." She grabbed his hand and pulled him along. "I am so excited. I never expected to find such an ideal place."

Her excitement dampened when she stood in the doorway and looked around the room. Layers of dust covered old furniture that filled half of the area. Trunks were stacked high in one corner to the ceiling. What appeared to be discarded household articles; old lamps, pictures, and empty frames filled every space and were piled every which way.

"Do you know any able bodied men who could help us move or dispose of all of this?" She gestured as she strolled around the room. "Today if possible."

"I have some mates who could 'elp. I mean help," Eel scratched his head.

"Very good, you learn very quickly." Nicola beamed and was rewarded with the biggest smile she had ever seen on Eel's face.

Nicola delighted in watching the boy carry his books, paper, pens, slate, and ink bottle with such care. They ate a late mid-day meal in Aunt Belle's kitchen as soon as they returned from their many errands.

"Does we start lessons today, miss?"

"After tea and for no more than two hours each day, Monday through Friday," Nicola replied. "The correct grammar is, 'do we start lessons,' not 'does we start lessons.'"

She listened while Eel pronounced the words.

"We must change into our work clothes before we clean the room. See if you can gather your mates. I will meet you back here."

Nicola hurried upstairs and changed her clothes. Before she went in search of cleaning supplies, she paused to examine Cook's burned arm. All the blisters were gone, and the redness had disappeared. The burn was healing as she knew it would. Nicola's herbal salve, once again, had done its job.

Retreating to her herbal room, her mind brimmed over with all she wanted to accomplish and of course, there was still Mr. Barber. He kept filtering into her thoughts. It took a great deal of concentration to keep him in the background, where he belonged. He moved around in her mind like an annoying, pesky fly, landing here and there. When she got rid of him in one place, he found another place to appear. He continued to make her remember feelings she had thought long buried in the past.

****

Eel had looked for Mr. Barber and Barnaby until late the previous evening but could not find either of them. He was worried and determined to seek them out tonight. Like yesterday, the feeling of being watched was there. He found no one when he doubled back, not once but three times. There was a lady who always seemed to be in the same shop or near the same place. She appeared to be shopping too. He watched her climb into a carriage and drive away.

Eel dashed home, changed clothes, and picked up his two mates, Jeb and Jimmy, on his way back to the Highbridge house.

Eel walked into the herbal room. "Miss Nicola, I be back and brung some help to clean the store room. I means the herbal room."

"The word is; 'mean' not 'means'. Oh, Eel, how wonderful. We can start to move furniture out today. I hope the men are big and strong." She spun around the room. "Where are they?"

"They be outside, miss."

"The correct word is 'are', not 'be'." Nicola moved toward the outside door.

"Wait," shouted the boy.

Nicola stopped.

"You see me—I have to explain." Eel looked down at the floor and shoved his hands in his pockets.

"What do you have to tell me?" Nicola pursed her lips together to keep from laughing at the lad's serious expression.

"I brung my friends, Jeb and Jimmy. They might not look like much but they will work hard." Pausing to catch his breath, he hurried to add, "I be hoping they could 'ave, I mean have lessons like me."

Nicola sighed.

Two more would not be any more trouble than one. All her life people had been willing to teach her. This would be her opportunity to give something back—to pass it forward to another generation.

"Well, Eel fetch your friends so we can get started."

The afternoon passed much too quickly. They moved all the smaller pieces of furniture out to the carriage house. Anything broken or in sad shape was put on the burn pile. The items left in the room were two trunks and a dresser too heavy for the lads to move.

They did manage to push those items into the far corner.

Tea arrived in short order. Sitting on the clean scrubbed floor, they had an indoor picnic. When Nicola's sister Mara arrived, Eel introduced Jeb and Jimmy. Acting like perfect gentlemen, the three lads shook her hand.

"Miss, be it time for our lessons now?" Eel asked.

"Yes, it is. We will have to get the table." Nicola pointed to the one sitting near the outside door. "Put it in the middle of the room and put five chairs around it."

"I am not staying. I will leave you to your classroom," Mara said. "Are you sure you want to do this? I did not think you planned on being in London long. Or has something changed I do not know about?"

"I enjoy helping others, and time will tell if I like being a teacher. I was a good student at one time." Nicola walked her sister to the door, which led into a hallway off the kitchen. "And no, I do not plan on being here long. I am here to help Emmy and that is all."

The three lads sat at the table like wooden soldiers. Eel unwrapped his books, supplies, and placed them on the center of the table. Nicola stood next to him.

"I am very happy to teach all of you. However, we do not have enough books or supplies. Tomorrow morning, the three of you will need to be here at ten sharp. We will go back to Ridgeway's Bookshop for more supplies."

"Miss, I…"

"Yes, Jeb?"

"I not be very bright, you see."

"You are a very smart young man." Nicola strolled over and patted his shoulder. "Everyone learns in different ways, and we will find the method most suited to you. You do the best you can. I promise no one"—she raised her eyebrows, turned, and looked down at Eel and Jimmy—"will laugh or make fun of you. Right, lads."

"Yes, miss." Both boys poked each other and started giggling.

****

Eel slipped away from Jeb and Jimmy as soon as they left the Highbridge house. It was essential he find Mr. Barber to ask about the follower.

He went first to the boarding house where George lived and confirmed he was still due back on Monday. Eel then hurried to Mr. Barber's house. He knocked on both the front and back door. No light came from any of the windows. He went to the side of the house and found a small window. Making sure no one could see him from the street, he opened it and climbed in.

He had discovered if he knew what was happening around him, his fear could never take hold of him. Worst case, if he knew who or what caused the distress, he could figure out how to avoid it.

The full moon cascaded light into the darkened house through the curtainless windows. While Eel waited for his eyes to adjust, he let his sense of smell lead him to a fireplace, which had recently been used. He stirred the ashes hoping to find some information that might have escaped the heat. His discovery was a warm firebox and nothing else. He wiped his hands, covered in soot, on his trousers and moved to the desk. He started to open the center drawer but stopped when he heard someone at the back door. Eel hurriedly retraced his steps, slid out the way he'd come in without making a sound, and shut the window. He ran to the back of the house and peeked around the corner as the door closed. He hastened to the library window, grabbed at the leafless vine growing on the broken trellis, and boosted himself up high enough to stand on a broken tree limb. All he saw was Barnaby sitting in the desk chair.

Eel sensed someone behind him, turned to look, and a large hand grabbed his trouser leg. He landed on the hard ground inches away from large black boots. Afraid, he sat staring at them.

"What the devil do you think you are doing?"

Eel jumped up and grabbed Mr. Barber in a joyful hug. "It be me, Mr. Barber. Eel."

"So I see. Come in the house. You do not have to peer in windows or sneak about." Mr. Barber motioned the boy to follow. "A knock on the door would do, you know. You are lucky you did not get shot or worse."

Eel stood, dusted off his backside, and trailed behind Mr. Barber. They went in the back door and hurried into the library. Clay caught him rubbing his bottom.

"Hit the ground a little hard?" Clay chuckled. "Serves you right for snooping."

"I been looking for you. I be 'ere earlier, and you was out. Saw the light, thought I be seeing who be in the 'ouse before I knocked me hand silly."

"Why were you looking for me? Has George come back?"

"I came to see you about the follower. I checked before I come here. George is still due back on Monday."

"All we could find out was someone at the museum

wanted the two of you followed. Do you know why?'

"It could be—"

"Still does not make sense why someone would follow either one of you." Clay walked around the room.

"I thinks someone followed us today. I doubled back a couple of times. A posh lady."

"Your imagination is running away with you, boy," Barnaby said. "We put the scare into the follower. Believe me he will not be back."

"Do not forget in five days we start our watch for your dear Uncle George. Meet you and your mates here at daybreak," Clay said.

"We be here," Eel announced, leaving the house. He let the door slam behind him. Eel walked for a block. He wasn't sure the men wouldn't figure out he had been in the house and come after him. He ran the rest of the way home. Eel wanted Jeb and Jimmy to watch wherever he and Miss Nicola traveled. Something was wrong. Everyone seemed to be hiding something. He would have to find out what the secrets were by himself.

After all, it be my job to protect Miss Nicola.

Chapter Six

"Do you get the feeling the boy ain't telling all?" said Barnaby. "There is something going on in the museum. I be thinking he and your lady have gotten themselves right smack in the middle of it."

"She is not my lady, damn it. We do not have the time to go rescuing the boy and a woman who should stay at home where she belongs." Clay stalked over to the desk. "Someone has been in the house. I—"

"Now your imagination is getting the best of you," Barnaby scolded.

Clay pointed to the center desk drawer. "The small piece of paper I placed on the side of the drawer could only have fallen on the floor if someone was looking for information." Barnaby and Clay stared at the small white fleck.

"I will go check the windows and doors." Barnaby hurried into the hallway.

"Whoever was here didn't find anything interesting because I burned every scrap of paper."

"Everything is in order. The only window which does not lock is too small for an adult to climb through. However, a child the size of Eel most likely could."

"I wonder if the boy was in the house." Clay ran his fingers through his hair. "He is too smart for his own good and ours."

"Eel is capable of something like that." Barnaby

moved toward the fireplace. He reached out his hand to feel the warmth, and then added more coal to the fire. "I agree he is smart, but why would he break in? It does not make any sense."

Clay watched the flames dance in the fireplace. That woman filled his thoughts. He had better things to think about.

****

Nicola thought the time she had to wait for Emmy to return would be dull and uneventful. It proved to be the exact opposite. Her parent search, her herbal study room, and the three young lads kept her busy. She always had numerous projects on her agenda. No task was too big or too small for her to take on. She could never say no if someone, anyone, needed her help.

As Nicola hurried out of Clark and Debenham's shop, an attractive ribbon display next to the entrance caught her attention, and she walked into the path of a passer-by. Her packages flew into the air. Only his tight grip on her arm steadied her and kept her from falling.

"Excuse me," said the man, as he released her. "Oh, it is you, Miss Highbridge." He smiled and stooped to retrieve the packages at his feet.

"Good morning, sir." Warmth filled her body. Rather than face Mr. Barber, she would have crawled under a large rock if one had been handy.

"I did not mean to run you down. I…" Clay's face turned red.

"Think nothing of it. I was looking at a display and not watching where I was going." She felt her face grow warm with embarrassment. "Eel, will you be a dear and help me please?" Plucking two packages out of Mr. Barber's hands, she put them into the boy's outstretched arms.

"Let me also be a dear and help you." Clay grinned. "I hope nothing is broken." He picked up two more packages. "You should not be carrying so many at one time."

She ignored his comments and walked toward the carriage she'd hired for the duration of her stay, which she estimated at a fortnight. Eel had recommended Yates and vouched for his honesty. The driver took charge of the rescued packages and placed them in the storage box at the back of the hackney. Mr. Barber assisted her into the carriage and climbed in after her.

"What do you think you are doing, sir?" She sat and pushed her back against the squabs in the carriage.

"I would like to talk with you. I have invited myself along." Clay sat directly across from her and tried to take her hand.

"You are very forward, sir." She moved her hands behind her back out of his reach.

"That may be. I need to discuss the follower with you." Leaning back, he crossed his arms over his chest, and glanced at Eel.

"You have my full attention." She tapped her feet lightly on the carriage floor, trying to keep her temper from showing.

"The weather does seem to be most pleasant today." Clay looked pleased with himself.

"Yes, Mr. Barber, it is. Now about the follower."

My fingers itch to wrap themselves around his neck and slowly squeeze until he turns blue. He is being—I have to think of a word to describe how annoying he can be.

"We will discuss this when we reach your

destination," Clay said.

"What if we have more shopping to do and are not going home?"

Clay looked out the window. "I can see your aunt's home, on the left, so it appears you are finished."

Eel opened the door and disappeared before the hackney came to a complete stop.

"I do wish he would stop jumping out of the carriage while it is moving." Nicola smoothed the wrinkles in her skirt.

"Why?" Clay asked, as the carriage door banged shut.

"He could injure himself." She released the breath she had been holding.

"Eel can take care of himself. Believe me."

Will that man ever agree with anything I say?

Yates helped Nicola out of the carriage. Jeb and Jimmy had kept a watchful eye by sitting on the luggage platform on the back. They jumped off and ran to the front door right behind Eel.

"We be ready to finish cleaning your herbal room now, miss," Jimmy said.

"I thought first we would have some tea and cakes. Unless you would rather start working?"

"No miss," Jimmy said, as Jeb jammed him hard in the ribs.

She turned toward the doorknocker to announce their arrival and stopped her hand in mid-air as the door swung open.

"Good afternoon, miss." Betsy curtsied.

"I already knocked," Eel said, with a huge grin.

"Well, thank you, young man." She handed her cape to the housemaid. "You lads, please go to the kitchen and stay out of Cook's way. I am going to speak to Mr. Barber. I will meet you in a few minutes."

The young boys thundered down the hallway toward the kitchen. Nicola and Clay moved into the sitting room and sat in green leafed chairs. A fire burned brightly. She wasn't sure if the chill she felt was from the weather or Mr. Barber.

"You want to talk about the man who followed Eel and me yesterday?"

"The two of you seem a doubtful pair for someone to follow."

"What you are saying is we are not worthy of being followed?"

"That is not what I mean. Do not put words in my mouth." Clay frowned. "It is my experience people are not followed unless they have something someone else wants—money, information, or some item of value."

"Oh, I see we are not of any value. Who would care—?"

"You are continuing to twist my words around."

"You have a great deal of experience in people following people?"

"No. I was in the war."

"It explains it all and yet nothing."

"I do not want to see either of you hurt, and I cannot follow you everywhere."

"Is that what you were doing today? Following us about, to see if we were followed. Well, cease and desist. I am sure someone was mistaken and thought we were more important than we are."

"I am only trying to protect you."

"Well, do not. I am not your responsibility, sir."

Nicola stood, hoping he would realize their

meeting had concluded. He too rose from his chair but made no move to leave. She started toward the door. *I can always push him out of the room, if he cannot take the hint.* After all there was work to be done. As she walked past him, he reached out and pulled her into his arms. In slow motion, his lips descended toward her upturned face.

She felt the jolt of current the minute their lips touched. It hummed through her entire body. His warm lips sent a pulsing heat. Her heartbeat quickened, and without thinking, she placed her arms around his neck, trying to pull him closer.

A knock on the closed door startled them both. They staggered apart, yet stood mere inches from each other. She touched her swollen lips and felt the warmth. Mr. Barber turned away from her. She opened the door and Jimmy ran in. Eel and Jeb sat on the stairs.

"Miss, we be wondering if Mr. Barber be able to help us move the heavy goods out of the herbal room?" Jimmy asked.

"I would be honored to help." Clay stood behind her and put his hand on her shoulder.

Nicola shivered as his warmth invaded her space. She wanted him to leave but instead found herself explaining what needed to be done. Once in the room, he issued commands to everyone. She could have left, and no one would have noticed.

They all decided—actually Mr. Barber decided—it would be best to have tea after the room was cleaned out. No task was too small or too large for the man to perform. The lads followed his instructions to the letter, and the room was emptied in minutes.

"What will this area be used for now it is cleaned

out?" Mr. Barber asked.

"Is goin' to be an herbal study room, ain't that right Miss Nicola?" Jimmy announced.

"Yes, Jimmy, you are right. I haven't had time to do as much studying of herbal remedies as I would like. While I am here, I shall spend most of my day doing that. There are a great many ills in this world, and I believe cures can be found if enough studying is done.

"You will not see people as part of your studies, will you?" Mr. Barber placed his hands on his hips. "It is not safe for a woman."

Sighing, Nicola pointed her finger in his direction. "I have been taught by the best and am not afraid of blood or even dying. Believe me, I am quite capable."

"I am sure you are. I was thinking more about the type of people here in London." Mr. Barber moved closer to her. "These are not honest country folks."

"What makes you think people who live in the country are honest? Two weeks ago a young man, the heir apparent, murdered his father." She bit her lip, to prevent her tears, as she remembered one of her favorite patients. "While I am here, I will offer my healing talents to anyone that comes for help."

She failed to mention the heir apparent also tried to kill her when she set about to prove to the authorities he killed his ailing father.

"Yes, but…" Mr. Barber turned to follow Nicola's movements across the room.

Their discussion ended when tea arrived. Mr. Barber seemed to think he could tell her what to do. Wait until he found out Nicola did as she pleased and answered to no one.

****

Determined not to let her sister disappear again, Nicola waited in Emmy's room late Sunday evening. She sat near the fire, her wool shawl thrown over her shoulders.

She wasn't sure what woke her, the thought of Mr. Barber kissing her again or the opening of the bedroom door when Emmy slipped in. Nicola sat in the shadows until her sister reached the center of the room.

"Welcome home, dear sister."

"Oh my!" Emmy jumped. "You scared the stuffing out of me. Now I have dropped my matches."

"I came here to help you, not take over." While Nicola waited for Emmy to appear, her eyes adapted to the darkness allowing her to reach down and retrieve the matches. "We are going to work on your dilemma together. The *we* refers to you, me, and Mara if necessary."

"You mean you do not have the thieves locked up?" Emmy shivered and moved toward the window. "I thought you would have taken care of it by now, or I would have stayed in Culworth." She reached up and removed the pins from the knot on the top of her head. Her hair cascaded past her shoulders and stopped beyond her waist.

Nicola lit all the lamps. She stirred the dying embers in the fireplace and added more coal to keep the wintery chill from creeping further into the room.

"You continue to amaze me. You thought all would be taken care of. I do not know what George looks like nor his last name. So pray tell, how could I go to the Runners and ask them to arrest someone I have never seen?" Nicola shook her head in disbelief at Emmy's foolish assumptions.

"Could we talk about this tomorrow morning? I am very tired." Emmy ran her fingers through her hair.

"No, Sister Dear. You are not going to sneak off somewhere in the morning before anyone wakes." Nicola sat back in the chair near the fireplace. "Did you forget? You have to go to the museum in the morning to complete your display."

"I want to take a bath and go to bed." Emmy tried to pull some of the tangles from her hair.

Nicola walked over and picked up a hairbrush from the dressing table.

"By all means, take your bath. I am not leaving until we discuss our plan of action and your part in it." Nicola yawned, handed the brush to Emmy, and settled back into the chair.

"I—"

A knock on the door interrupted Emmy. The upstairs maid, Sally, arrived with fresh towels. Betsy, the housemaid, followed with two buckets of hot water, which she poured into the tub at the side of the fireplace, then hurried back into the hallway and returned with two more steaming buckets.

"Miss Emmy, I be assisting with your bath?" Sally asked.

"It is not necessary." Nicola spoke up. "I will assist her."

The servants left the room without making a sound.

"Nicola really I…" Emmy bit her bottom lip and looked at the floor.

"We either talk now, or I return to Chew Magna in the morning."

Emmy's head jerked up.

"I will leave, and you can handle George."

Nicola had no intention of leaving London, at least not yet. She had unfinished business with Mr. Barber. Her fingers touched her lips. Her innermost yearnings bubbled to the surface when she thought of a future with a husband who would love her and children. She just had to identify her birth parents, because without family roots a future with Mr. Barber, or any other gentleman, was impossible.

"All right, all right." Emmy sighed and her shoulders slumped.

Nicola stayed in the chair and enjoyed the warmth of the fire as her sister undressed, stomped around the room, and got in the tub.

Emmy is trying to figure a way to have 'Sister Dear', me, take over, as usual. Well, not this time. I will not be controlled by anyone, especially my sister.

But Nicola couldn't stop Mr. Barber from popping into her thoughts. She was learning to tolerate his interruptions, which thus far proved to be very pleasurable. She closed her eyes and enjoyed the pictures of his kiss running through her mind.

"Nicola, oh, Nicola, have you fallen asleep? You said we need to talk. Well, I am waiting."

Like I have been waiting for you. "I have been in deep thought." Nicola ran her tongue over her lips.

"About what or should I say about whom? Your voice just now had a dreamy quality to it. Are you sure you weren't thinking of Mr. Barber?"

"Back to the problem at hand," Nicola said. "Your note was delivered to the museum. Lord Willforde is expecting you in the morning at your usual time."

Nicola did not mention the man in the library, the mystery follower, or Mr. Barber, and friend. It was best

Emmy didn't know everything.

"I expect George to seek you out immediately. Here is what I think"—Nicola pointed to Emmy and then herself—"you and I should do."

Emmy listened, shook her head a few times, but agreed to the plan. Satisfied her sister understood what they needed to do. Nicola helped her out of the bath and tucked her into bed.

"I am going to say this once more. I have come to help you, but you must do your part. We—you, Mara and I—are in this together. We may be foster sisters, but we are family. No secrets and no running away. No matter what. Understood?"

"Yes, Nicola."

"We promise to take care of each other and to help you through the difficulty you are facing." Nicola took Emmy's coin, put it in her sister's open palm, and folded her hand over it. "I, Nicola Highbridge, make this pledge. Your turn, Emmy."

Emmy sighed. "I vow to do my part in assisting you, Nicola, with my crisis."

"You keep your coin with you for providence. I will see you in the morning for breakfast. Do not leave the house without me." Nicola gathered her shawl and draped it over her shoulders. "I have a few more ideas I want to discuss with you and Mara before we depart for the museum."

"I promise to see you at breakfast," Emmy said. "So you know I would much rather be going back to Culworth."

Nicola moved across the room and extinguished the lamps, except for the one by the four poster bed. Emmy always had been afraid of the dark and insisted a lamp be left burning throughout the night.

Nicola sighed and closed the door behind her. She wished she could return home and be done with Emmy and her problem until Mr. Barber, and his kiss, once again filled her thoughts.

Chapter Seven

The sky, a gray blanket of clouds, cast its gloom into the room early the next morning. Strolling to the windows, Nicola touched her fingertips to one of the panes of glass. The cold could mean snow, which she preferred over rain.

Smoked ham sizzled to perfection, freshly baked scones, and brewed tea summoned her into the breakfast room. She was going to have to order some coffee, which was her favorite early morning beverage.

Nicola's face brightened when she saw Mara sitting at the table eating. She rushed over to greet her, reached down, and hugged her. "You look fabulous as always." Nicola strolled over to the sideboard where the breakfast buffet had been placed. "Where is Aunt Belle? I do not want her overhearing our conversation."

"It is quite safe. She is never up until mid-morning," Mara said. "Besides, we saved you a seat where you can watch for her." Mara pointed to the head of the table, which had a clear view of the door.

Nicola gathered her breakfast choices and sat at the table with Mara on one side and Emmy on the other. Between bites of food, she outlined her plan for Mara's benefit.

"How is Catherine doing?" Nicola stood to get another cup of tea. She was always eager for news of Catherine Highbridge, their foster mother, who still lived in Milborne Port where they had all grown up.

"She is wonderful and beautiful as always," Mara said. "I went to visit her two weeks ago when I delivered the new dresses she ordered. She is one of my best customers."

"Remember, the time we dressed up in her old gowns and put on face powder her maid gave us?" Emmy piped up.

"How could I forget?" Mara said. "It took my face a week to recover from the scrubbing, which I always thought was worse than your punishment."

"You had on more than we did. In fact if I remember right your face was almost white." Nicola laughed and Emmy joined in.

Mara always complained she received the worst reprimand, while in truth she managed to talk her way out of any trouble the three women found themselves in.

"Emmy, are you about ready to leave?" Nicola asked.

"Yes, pray, let me finish breakfast. Oh, botheration." Emmy pushed her plate away. "I cannot eat another bite I am so…"

"I know you are frightened." Nicola patted Emmy's arm. "Remember I am coming with you."

"Will someone like George think it is odd you are with Emmy?" Mara asked.

"No. Emmy wants to show her older sister where she toils over her ancient ones. It will give me a good chance to see the entire layout of the museum. You never know. Someday I might be on my own in the cavernous building."

The sound of the door opening alerted the women,

and all conversation stopped.

"She never comes down for breakfast. It is always served in her room," Mara whispered, knowing Aunt Belle couldn't hear her.

"Your information is flawed." Nicola suppressed a giggle.

"I know gels, I should still be asleep. I knew the three of you would be here, early in the morning. I do so love having all of you together. So here I am." Aunt Belle sat at the table. Her maid brought her breakfast.

The conversation turned to Nicola's wardrobe, or rather the lack of one. Mara agreed to bring some clothes home, and between the four of them, they came up with some fashionable ideas. Nicola's only interest was in the serviceability of her clothes. She decided to let Mara and Aunt Belle have their fun. Nicola tried to look enthused, but in truth she was bored as always when it came to discussing fashion. Mara always looked so proper, never a strand of blonde hair out of place nor any dirt smudged on her clothing. Unfortunately Nicola was the opposite.

In fact, Nicola would never forget a picnic when she and Mara had been sitting next to each other on a blanket watching the boat races. When it was time to leave, Nicola found she was the one with fresh mud on her dress. Mara of course had no dirt anywhere on her person.

Nicola and Emmy left them discussing clothes, fashion, and the *Ton*, which appeared to be Aunt Belle's favorite subject. Nicola thought of Eel, and wondered why she wouldn't be seeing him today.

"Miss Nicola, me has a previous engagement. I can't be breaking it," he had said.

Intrigued, Nicola thought most of the time the boy was an adult in a child's body. He was worldly in many ways and acted so mature at times. It was easy to forget he was a child, a young lad who had seen more than he should have for his age.

Yates drove straight to the museum. There would be no sightseeing this cloudy day.

"You know, Nicola." Emmy settled herself back against the squabs. "I am enjoying this ride. It is so nice having a hired driver. I always found it quite impossible to find a hackney for hire at this hour."

"I will miss my daily regimen of walking, which I have discovered to be good exercise. Until this situation is well in hand, it is better not to be out and about on our own."

Yates helped them down when they reached the museum and walked them to the front. He had no problem opening the heavy door.

****

"What in the bloody hell is she doing here?" Clay mumbled.

"Talking to yourself are you now?" Barnaby hunkered down next to him.

"Where did George go?" Clay clenched his jaw as he turned to his friend.

"He went into the museum. I left Eel and friends watching the three back doors."

"Are you sure all the doors are covered?" Clay tried his best not to sound as annoyed as he felt.

"Yes, one door leads to the kitchen area, one is an exit from the library, and one from the side of the museum. No one can leave from the back or side of the building without the lads seeing them."

"I still wonder…" Clay paused.

"Who and what are you talking about?"

"Her. Miss Nicola Highbridge."

Barnaby raised his eyebrows. "Maybe you should ask Eel? He might know."

It was a good thing Barnaby had told Clay where the lad was hiding because when he tried to locate him he couldn't.

"Eel come out. I need to talk to you," Clay whispered, near the stack of wooden crates.

One minute Clay was by himself and the next, the boy stood beside him.

"I just saw your other employer." Clay paused.

"Me what?" Eel whispered. "Oh, you mean Miss Nicola."

"She went into the museum with another woman, her sister. I think." Clay rubbed his gloveless hands together to keep them warm. He would have to stop at the emporium once again and purchase gloves. He was forever misplacing them. This time he'd left them in the carriage.

"What's her doing 'ere, I mean here?" Eel asked.

"I was hoping you could explain." Clay continued to glance around to make sure no one was watching them.

"I know Miss Emmy—'er be employed at the museum."

"She what?"

"'Er works."

"I know what you said, but women do not work in a museum." Clay rubbed the stubble on his chin. "Women stay or *should* stay at home where they belong."

"Miss Emmy be an expert and digs up old Roman things. Her makes special displays in the museum."

"The day you and Miss Nicola were followed, you never mentioned visiting her sister." Clay's voice carried the confusion he felt.

"We delivered a note to the gent in charge of the place for Miss Emmy." Eel paused. "Miss Nicola wanted to look up a design on a ring too. Something to do with her family—" Eel moved from foot to foot. The wind was picking up and blowing hard where he stood.

"You mean a signet ring?"

"That be it." Eel nodded.

"I wonder why she would be looking for a signet ring design." Clay jammed his hands into his coat pockets. "Did she say?"

"No, sir."

"Well, back to your post. Either Barnaby or I will come later to relieve you."

A large wagon turned from a side road and approached the back of the museum to make a delivery. Clay glanced back to tell Eel and realized the boy was gone. He shook his head. The lad continued to amaze him.

I wonder what my sons would be like, if I ever had any. I cannot believe I am even thinking of such nonsense. To have a real family, I would have to be married. I never plan to be leg-shackled to any woman. I don't care if my numbskull cousin inherits after I am dead and buried.

He only had to think about his married mates, who had become the dullest of companions since their weddings, to reinforce his thoughts on wedded bliss. The men had changed, becoming old doddering fools chasing after their wives from one party to the next. Gone were the intellectual conversations, replaced by talk of fashion, marriage, babies, and gossip. He found the thought of marriage distasteful.

Being careful not to make a sound, he moved back around to the side of the building where the delivery was taking place. He wanted to catch a glimpse of what was going on.

He discovered when he began his government career if he acted like he belonged, most people thought he did. The tactic had saved him more than once during the war. He walked closer and watched, while workers unloaded the wagon. It was impossible to guess the contents in the crates. The writing on them was unreadable from this distance. The containers were all different sizes; from small ones one person could carry, to large ones that took two to three men to unload.

Why would George work in a museum? Where do the Highbridge ladies fit into the big puzzle? A very large piece seemed to be floating just out of his view.

He smiled, thinking of Nicola until the wagon moved down the side road and back onto the main road toward Barnaby. Eel would have to find Nicola. He must learn why she was in the museum before she ruined his carefully laid plans. When she showed up, anything could happen.

Chapter Eight

Eel heaved open the museum door enough to squeeze through. Mr. Pagger stood at his guard post in the lobby.

"I say, boy, children are not allowed unless accompanied by an adult."

He straightened his shoulders and stared at Mr. Pagger. "I be here to meet Miss Highbridge. Her be expecting me."

"Well, I do suppose you can wait right here. You will not dash off by yourself. Do I make myself clear? It is just not done." He pointed his nose in the air, as he pushed his glasses in place.

Eel lost his patience with the milksop and turned to leave. He stopped short of running smack into Lord Willforde.

"Young man, have we not met before?" The museum curator asked. "A few days ago, before the weekend if I am not mistaken. It is a pleasure to see you again." He put out his hand and Eel shook it. "I just saw your Miss Highbridge with the museum's Miss Highbridge. Come with me, and we shall find them." He tapped Mr. Pagger's arm to get his attention. "This young man, Eli, can come into the museum any time he likes and can go anywhere he likes. Do you understand me?"

"Yes, sir." Mr. Pagger removed his glasses and

marched down the hallway.

"Eli, I must apologize. Mr. Pagger continues to…Well, I will take care of him later."

Lord Willforde took Eel on a guided tour of all the areas they passed. There were statues of Greek Gods, and Egyptian artifacts from the tomb of a forgotten pharaoh whose name Eel couldn't begin to pronounce. He tucked his hands into his pockets to keep from touching the wonderful treasures. He was so absorbed in his surroundings everything else was forgotten.

They moved behind the scenes, into the storage areas and workrooms. The smell of turpentine, varnish, paint, dust, and mildew made his nose itch. He found these areas as interesting as the actual displays. A door swung open as two men dragged a wooden box into the hallway. They followed the men into a large area where boxes were being shuffled from place to place.

"I found you, Miss Nicola." Eel ran to her.

"What a pleasant surprise. I thought you were to be engaged most of the day." Nicola touched his arm and gave it a gentle squeeze.

"Yes, miss, but me plans changed." He grinned at her. "So I came to 'elp as promised."

"I do not remember you—"

"Lord Willforde, he be giving me a tour while we was looking for you." He spun around in a circle. "This be a wonderful place."

"Emmy gave me a tour too." Nicola took Eel's hand in hers. "You are right. It is wondrous. I could spend hours here."

"Miss Emmy, one of them new crates that arrived be bashed in on one side. Before it can be moved off the dock, you need to inspect it," one of the workers said.

"I would prefer to examine it later." Emmy glanced in Nicola's direction.

"Miss Highbridge, go look at the crate with George." Lord Willforde said. "I will stay with your sister and Eli until you return." He took Nicola's elbow in a firm grip and led her to one of the newly unpacked statues. Emmy and George walked in the opposite direction.

"Where is Eli?" Lord Willforde turned to Nicola.

****

A blast of cold air greeted Emmy as George pushed her through the door to the outside dock.

"Thought you could hide from me?" George took a hard hold of Emmy's arm and spun her around. "Well, you does what I say or accidents start happening." He made a slashing gesture across his throat.

"You cannot do this. Nicola will stop you." Emmy tried to pull her arm free. George tightened his grip. "You are nothing but a common thief. I refuse to help."

"You do as I say or else." He raised his hand to strike her.

Eel, hidden among the half opened crates of statues and books, grabbed a small wooden box and hurled it through the air. It hit George's arm, bounced across the floor stopping when it slammed into a large barrel filled with packing material. The box shattered on impact.

Before George could again take aim at Emmy, Eel jumped and grabbed George around his shoulders to stop him from striking her.

"Run, Miss Emmy, run," Eel hollered.

Emmy screamed and ran for the door.

Eel flew through the air the moment George's fist

connected with his jaw. He bit the inside of his cheek, and his mouth filled with blood. The copper taste made him gag forcing the red liquid to run down his chin. Eel tried to move and watched through a haze as George vaulted over a mound of loose packing material, crashed through a partially opened door, and disappeared by jumping off the dock. Eel managed to stretch his legs out straight and tried to push himself into a sitting position. He fell backward and was plunged into darkness.

****

Eel felt cold water dribbling down his neck, as he began to open his eyes. A small lamp perched on a table emitted a thin sliver of light. With great care, he reached up and felt a cold cloth, which lay across his forehead. He turned his head and realized Miss Nicola, her eyes closed, sat next to him.

He tried to ease himself upright but became nauseated, and lowered his head back to the couch.

"Eel, please do not move too fast," Nicola said. "Lord Willforde wishes you to remain here until the doctor he has summoned arrives."

"But miss, you be a healer." Eel closed his eyes until the flash of pain in his head lessened. "Did George get away?"

"Yes, I am afraid he did. Now you lie still."

"But miss, I have to go outside and talk to Mr. Barber."

"Mr. Barber? Please, Eel, rest and you will be fine in no time."

She walked back to Lord Willforde's office to see why the doctor hadn't yet arrived.

"How is our young lad, miss?"

"He will be fine, Lord Willforde. He has a concussion, bruising on his face and ribs, and a cut on the inside of his cheek. He is a little confused at the moment."

"I am grateful you understand about calling for a real…" Lord Willforde blushed and looked at his feet. "The museum after all is responsible." His eyes never left his buckled shoes.

The doctor came and gave him the same diagnosis Nicola had. Feeling smug, she walked out of Willforde's office.

Doctor Cooper hadn't been so full of himself and agreed with the treatment she proposed.

She gave the good doctor Aunt Belle's address. Eel would convalesce there; the doctor could visit every day and report back to Lord Willforde.

Willforde couldn't believe George was responsible for the thievery and sent for the Runners to report the robberies. He planned to hire Bow Street to find George and hopefully recover the stolen items. Many of the articles were priceless and couldn't be replaced.

"Miss Emmy, I am truly sorry about your ordeal. I wish you had come to me," Lord Willforde said, patting Emmy's arm as she and Nicola stood next to him in the hallway.

"I contacted the one person I knew I could trust— my sister." Emmy looked directly at Nicola.

"Miss Nicola." Eel walked unsteadily into the hallway toward them. "I be wanting to leave now. Please."

"We will leave soon." Nicola hurried to his side. "You, however, are not, I repeat not, going to walk to the carriage."

A chair mysteriously appeared. Nicola gently pushed Eel into it.

"I did not hurt me legs, just me head."

"I know, but we must wait for the Runners to come. It would be best if you lie down."

"Yes, miss." Eel sighed, weary beyond words.

Nicola and Emmy helped him back to the makeshift bed in the small room and covered him with a light blanket. He stared at the ceiling while Nicola tucked him in.

The steady sound of boots tramping on the wooden floor in the hallway echoed and sounded like an army of men.

Chapter Nine

"Emmy, you stay with Eel."

Emmy nodded her head, tears running down her face. "Eel, you could have been killed coming to my aid." She touched his hand. "I am so sorry you have been injured."

Emmy rushed to sit in the chair near the settee. Nicola didn't have time to comfort her. She opened the door and found Mr. Barber in the hallway with three other men.

Clay tried to hide his surprise. "I should have known you would be in the middle of this." He clenched his hands into fists so he wouldn't be tempted to shake her.

"What are you doing here? I do not recall anyone inviting you." Nicola was surprised when her resentment at his appearance turned to a sudden pleasure at seeing him.

"Come, come, let us go to the office across the hall." Lord Willforde looked at the four men and Miss Nicola. "We have grave business to discuss."

Nicola followed the men and Willforde into a tiny office. The room was small but managed to hold six people. She tried to stand near the window but was forced, by the confines of the room, to stand directly in front of Mr. Barber.

She stood so close she could feel his breath from

her head to her toes, as it caressed her body. A flame began a slow burn in her center. The longer they stood together the more liquid her knees became.

"I am Clay Barber. I have met Miss Nicola, but not you, sir." He inched past her toward Lord Willforde and shook hands.

She tried to shift her body but was forced to lean against the inside wall, in an attempt to bring her body temperature down and stay composed.

"I am looking for my young helper," Clay said. "He was to meet me in front of the museum. I became concerned when I saw all the activity."

"Mr. Barber, I sadly believe your young helper has been injured." Willforde then told the story of Eli's bravery in rescuing Emmy, of George's brutality, and the thievery.

"Lord Willforde, I do not think George worked alone," Clay said. "I would not be surprised if you find a few more people missing from your staff come morning."

"Eli is a very brave lad," Lord Willforde said.

"Who pray is Eli and where is Eel?" Clay frowned at Nicola.

"Eel is Eli," she said, with a trace of laughter in her voice. "Eli is his given name which he does not often use. He prefers to be called Eel."

"I must say Eel is a very unusual name," Lord Willforde said.

"Believe me, Eel is the perfect name for the lad." Clay shook his head. "He is artful and can be as slippery as an eel, when he needs to be."

Everyone turned as the door opened and the boy walked into the room, his face ashen.

"I tried to stop him. He would not listen to me," Emmy said, wringing her hands as she hurried in.

"This young man needs to be in bed." Clay picked him up. "I will carry him down to the carriage."

At the door Willforde stopped them. "Eli, thank you again for saving Miss Emmy. I will come to see you next week to discuss your reward."

"I not be needing no reward, sir."

"That may be young man, but we will meet." Willforde patted Eel's arm. My carriage is waiting at the front entrance. I must continue my discussion with the Runners."

The ladies followed behind Clay and Eel. Jeb stood next to the carriage. Tears ran down his face. "He ain't dead, is he miss?"

"No Jeb, he is not dead." Nicola knelt down and looked into his eyes. "He got hurt saving Miss Emmy from harm. He will be fine in a few days."

"It be George, miss?"

"How did you know—?"

"Jeb, ride on the back of the carriage, NOW!" Clay barked.

Nicola noticed the infuriated look Jeb received from Mr. Barber as the boy moved where he'd been told.

"Was that necessary? The child is frightened enough. You did not have to make it worse."

Helped by the driver, Clay lifted Eel into the carriage. He made a bed for him on one side, which allowed the ladies to sit across from the boy. Clay positioned himself between the women and was much too close for Nicola's comfort. Her skin grew warm and tingled when his thigh brushed against her knee.

The dress shop closed for the remainder of the day. Jimmy and Jeb delivered messages to all the customers canceling their appointments.

After much discussion it was decided Susan, Eel's mother, would also stay at Aunt Belle's home. The shop would open tomorrow, as usual, but in the evening, Susan would stay in the room next to her son's. It had a connecting door, and if Eel needed her, he could ring the bell on the nightstand, next to his bed. Nicola would be down the hall and could be summoned as well.

For the first two days, Eel slept a great deal. On the third day, he awoke with a clear head and sat up in bed.

"I have a great deal to tell you," Nicola said. "Eat all your breakfast and take a short nap."

"Why do I have—?"

"Only then will I tell you all that has happened."

Nicola escaped to her herbal study room in search of anything to occupy her mind, besides the happenings at the museum. What possible connection could Eel, George, Emmy, and Clay have had that brought them all together? Or was it happenstance?

She left open the hallway door and took a deep breath of the wonderful aromas of the busy kitchen preparing for the day's meals. The smell of yeast, flour, and the bread baking grabbed her attention. The thought of one slice of the bread fresh from the oven smothered with creamy rich butter and topped with blackberry preserves made her hungry. Although she couldn't always understand the servants, their happy voices and laughter gave her a sense of comfort.

A knock on the outside door brought her back to her task. She called out, "Please enter," as she moved away from the small desk covered with dried herbs in the corner of the room. A very tall, thin man stood in the entrance. Nicola tilted her head back to look at his weather-beaten and emaciated face.

"Miss." His eyes scanned the room. "I be from Bow Street, Ned Gold." His right arm had a blood-soaked rag wrapped around it several times. "I done 'urt me arm. A fellow Runner said for me to come 'ere for 'elp?"

"You have come to the right place." Nicola motioned him in and pointed to the table in the center of the room.

He stooped to lower his tall frame through the doorway and sat in the chair closest to the entrance. He first tried putting his feet flat on the floor, but his knees didn't fit under the table's edge. His body was too far away for Nicola to examine his arm on a flat surface. He finally thrust his feet out straight, which made it appear he had been poured into the chair.

Nicola scrubbed her hands with hot water from the kitchen pot. She steeped lavender, plantain, and primrose in a small bowl and cleaned the three-inch knife wound with the mixture. She sewed it closed with small even stitches. Ned kept his eyes closed the entire time, never moved, and never made a sound.

"You should keep your arm immobile until the stitches are removed."

"Cannot be doing that." He opened his eyes. "No work, no pay. Got me a family to feed."

She strained the warm water from the bowl. A small cloth filtered the herbs while the medicinal water poured into a glass jar. She placed the compress right on the gash. The plant properties would aid in the healing of the wound: lavender to prevent infection, plantain to prevent inflammation and ease the pain, and primrose for general healing.

"Come back in seven days to have the stitches removed. And take some clean bandages because you need to change the dressing every day." She motioned to the jar. "Dip a small bandage in this solution and place it on the wound. Cover it with a fresh cloth. It is very important. It will keep your wound clean. Otherwise your arm can become infected. If you need more bandages, come back. I will provide them."

Ned left some coins on the table, picked up his herbal supplies. "Thank you, miss."

Nicola smiled and walked him to the door. She kept a written record on each person she saw which allowed her to gather the necessary information to start a detailed study of health problems in London.

Word of mouth traveled fast, and Nicola found more people coming to her door for cuts, burns, rashes, and broken bones. There were few doctors who would see people without funds to pay for services rendered. Her morning became very busy. It gave her great joy to do her life's work. Being able to help someone in pain and offer comfort gave her a sense of accomplishment. It was the one place Mr. Barber didn't enter her mind and left her in peace, well at least most of the time.

Betsy came to tell her it was time for her noon meal. She locked the door and went into the kitchen. It hadn't taken people long to realize if they needed her, all they were required to do was knock on the kitchen door. The cook would send someone to find her.

She joined the happy voices in the kitchen, sat at the table, and ate not one but two pieces of hot, buttered bread smothered in preserves and honey. The servants' laughter was contagious. Aunt Belle treated her servants with respect. Nicola was reluctant to leave but knew Eel would be waiting to hear about George and the museum.

She found him in his room, sitting in a chair near the window. He appeared to be observing the street activities until she realized he was asleep. He look so very young, and yet so old.

She shuddered to think of what could have happened to Emmy if Eel hadn't been there, and said a thankful prayer. They, the Highbridge family, owed this young man more than they could ever repay.

"Miss, you been 'ere long? I fell asleep again. It be all I do."

She sat down next to him. "Your body is healing itself while you sleep. Do not fret, it will last but a short time. I thought we could talk about—"

"I needs to go to the screen. I ate me breakfast and me noon meal. Every bite, like you said. I be wanting to 'ear about George."

"The words are, 'need' not 'needs' and, 'my' not 'me,'" Nicola said, helping him up from the chair.

Eel repeated the words.

She guided him to the screen. While Eel did the necessary, she fixed his bedding. He had progressed halfway across the room when she looked up from her task. She helped him into bed. To her relief, his face had gained more natural color, and his eyes were clear and bright, regardless of the rings of colors around them. He should be back to normal within another day or two.

She told him about George and closely scrutinized

his face. "You know, Eel, I wonder how you knew George's name." Nicola sat on the edge of the bed. "What made you hide in the storeroom? Could you explain it all to me?"

"Well, miss, hum—hum—"

Voices echoed down the hallway. One belonged to Mara and the other to Doctor Cooper, as the sound was too deep for any of the women's voices, and she knew it wasn't Mr. Barber. Nicola looked at Eel for a few moments before the door opened. "We will continue this discussion later."

Chapter Ten

"Good afternoon, Miss Highbridge, Eel. I knew I would find our lad still stuck in this old bed."

"If you will excuse me, I must be off." Mara shut the door.

Doctor Cooper moved over to the bed where Eel sat like a young king viewing his subjects. The doctor took his hand, checked his pulse, then his face, looked at his eyes, and then the lump on the back of his head.

"Have you been up and about young man?"

"Miss Nicola just helped me back to bed. I sat in the chair and fell asleep."

"How are you feeling? You must be honest with me now."

"Feeling better, but tired. I be awake. Then I be waking up, never remember falling asleep."

"You were hurt badly. A few more days in bed and you will be good as new." The doctor touched Eel's head. "Miss Highbridge and I will leave you to rest."

"I will be back later to continue our discussion." Nicola shut the door.

The boy is trying to hide something. I will find out what.

"I say, Miss Highbridge."

She focused on the good doctor while they walked down the hallway.

"I understand you are a herbal healer. I wonder if

83

you would discuss what type of work you do, and for whom."

Nicola couldn't tell if anger or interest were in his voice as she couldn't see his face.

"Of course I am more than willing to share my herbal activities with you." She learned long ago to face adversity head on. She couldn't and wouldn't hide what she was nor what she did.

She led the way to her herbal room and stopped in the kitchen long enough to take the boiling kettle of water with her. The cook kept a kettle or pan full at all times. Nicola never knew when she would need hot water. Her training had taught her hot water—hot as she could stand—was best used to kill parasites and germs. Hand washing was done often, and all utensils were submerged in hot water after they were used. She credited her many successes to her cleanliness.

She invited Doctor Cooper to sit at the table, while she made tea. While it steeped, she showed him her stores of herbs and discussed in some detail what she believed her role to be in the healing process.

"Where did you learn your herbal training?"

"The gypsies were my greatest teachers. A group stayed on my foster mother's property every year." She brushed the tendrils of hair away from her face. "As a child I became fascinated with their costumes and customs. Their healer made me her apprentice." She served tea. "I also learned from local healers and anyone I or my foster mother could find."

"I always thought gypsies were thieves and—I thought they were nothing but trouble."

"In any group of people, there are some that make the rest look unscrupulous. But as a whole, they are loyal, and family is most important to them." She sipped her tea. "They do what they believe they must to survive."

She poured more tea into their cups from an old teapot she had rescued from the trash heap. The small cat on the lid reminded her of "Fiddles" her favorite childhood pet. Aunt Belle offered to buy her a new pot, but Nicola preferred the old Wedgwood creamware.

"Were you never afraid they would steal you away from your family?"

Nicola chuckled. "Many of them were not pleased I was being taught the gypsy herbal secrets handed down since time began. I was let into their inner circle, which was most unusual, and frightened many of them."

"I must admit I have never spoken to a gypsy. Not a true one. They made me much too uncomfortable." Doctor Cooper leaned back in his chair. "When I see their caravans, I make a point to go the other way."

"They can be intimidating if they choose." Nicola's voice filled with laughter. "Believe me. When I was about six and ten, a new gypsy caravan camped on our property for the first time. They were a large group, forty in number give or take a few who seemed to wander in and out." Remembering, she stood and took her red herbal healing bag from the cupboard. "Catherine, my foster mother, required the leader of any group to come and let her know where they were staying, and for how long, and the numbers in their group."

"I cannot believe a sensible woman would allow such a thing," said the doctor. "Did the local people complain?"

"Catherine said she needed to know where they

were staying, so she could help protect them from local people, who of course objected. They stayed on her property, so the local gentry had to live with it. She took full responsibility for them.

"Yes, my dear, but…" Doctor Cooper shook his head in disbelief.

"The wind blew so hard one stormy winter night anything not tied down flew through the air. Tree limbs blocked many of the roads." She lowered her voice to a whisper and gripped the edge of the table. "Someone pounded on the front door and woke the entire house." She paused and laughed. "Well, everyone except my sister, Mara. She could sleep through the world ending."

"I am sure it was most frightening." The doctor reached toward her.

Nicola moved her hands into her lap, out of his view. "In truth, no. It meant someone needed our help. To make a long story short, a gypsy prince had been thrown from his horse and seriously hurt. The local doctor refused to attend him. His guard feared he would die. Someone remembered I had been trained by a healer from another caravan." She shrugged her shoulders. "Their old healer had died a few months before the accident." She paused. "Any way, they came for my assistance."

"Do you mean to tell me your foster mama let you help them?" He again shook his head showing his disapproval.

"Of course. Healing doesn't care about color of someone's skin, race, or religion."

He frowned and pursed his lips. "I am vexed at your foster mama's ideas."

"Catherine happens to be a forward thinking woman. She raised three babies when their parents didn't want them. Someday the world's ideas will catch up with hers." She stopped to take a breath and a drink of her cooling tea. "Back to my story. I gathered all my supplies and went to their camp where I stayed for a fortnight. The prince survived. For a few days, I couldn't be sure he would. The gypsy tribe gave me this bag for my supplies." She opened it.

The doctor gasped in surprise.

The leather was soft and dark red. One side of the bag had fur-lined compartments. Each one held a labeled bottle. Peter removed the first one. The ingredient, lavender, was neatly printed on the label. He put it back and looked at another. The other side of the bag had larger compartments, also fur-lined. These held scissors, knives, needles, and small splints. The center of the bag held bandages.

"Every year or two the gypsies come to stay and repay their debt by offering to do whatever needs to be done. They fix the roof, paint the house; there is always something that needs to be fixed or repaired."

"To say I am astonished to hear such a story is an understatement. I will have to rethink my idea of gypsies."

To her surprise she found the doctor to be interested in her herbal medicines. All doctors used herbs in their practices, but many felt herbal healers were a threat.

"Miss Highbridge, I would like to learn whatever you are willing to teach me about the herbs you use."

She was taken aback. "When do you want to start?"

"Now is a good time?"

She laughed along with him.

"Let us decide on a plan. I will be sure and cover all the information you want. It will be easier for me to do and for you to remember."

"I agree. My name is Peter Cooper. We will be working associates. I hope we will become friends. Please call me Peter."

"I will agree to that, if you will call me Nicola."

****

Clay raised the front door knocker.

"Good afternoon, sir," said Sally, opening the door. "Miss Nicola be in the herbal study room with the doctor. I be pleased to show you the way." She curtsied.

"Thank you. First I would like to see Eel."

The minute Clay walked in, Eel's eyes lit up.

"Did you catch George?"

Clay put his fingers to his lips and then closed the door. "No we didn't. How are you feeling?"

"Not being treated like a baby anymore," Eel said, as he sat up straighter. "Gets up and does the necessary by myself. Don't need no one to 'elp me." A red blush washed across the boy's face. "Tell me about George?"

"Barnaby and Jimmy followed him when he ran out of the museum, but the thief realized someone was pursuing him. He bolted into an empty warehouse along the river. Barnaby and Jimmy could not keep him in sight."

"But Jimmy, he knows the area. I wonder," Eel said.

"You are too smart for your breeches." Clay grinned and touched Eel's shoulder. "Two burly gents, looking and acting like guards, appeared at one of the entrances. Barnaby and Jimmy were forced to retreat."

"Them ware'ouses are going to be torn down to make way for new buildings? Might you check to see who owns them?" Eel asked, excitement gleaming in his eyes.

"As I said, too smart for your own good. Barnaby is checking the ownership as we speak." Clay pulled a chair closer to the bed and sat on it. "He is looking through the records. You get some rest. I am going to find Miss Nicola. I will be back tomorrow, and hopefully, take you for a ride in my carriage. You look like you need some fresh air." He started toward the door.

"Wait, Miss Nicola has been asking questions about George. What should I be telling 'er?"

Clay turned back to Eel. "That woman needs to stay out of my business. Tell her you overheard her and Miss Emmy talking. Rest and I'll see you tomorrow."

****

Clay stood unnoticed in the herbal room doorway. He wasn't too keen on the way the doctor looked at Nicola. He did like the way she held her own, like Eel. She wasn't afraid of much. Her knowledge of herbs and medicine in general was impressive. A sense of pride stole over him as he listened to her talk. Why should he care about a slip of a woman who didn't act much like a lady?

There she was, entertaining the fine doctor. *I could shake her until she rattles she makes me so...always butting into my business, messing up my mind. She should be upstairs watching over Eel, and wringing her hands about the injustice of it all.*

"It sure does smell good in here." He knocked on

the open door.

Nicola and the doctor were examining some dried rosemary, their heads inches apart. They jerked up the moment Clay spoke.

"Who invited you?" Nicola asked.

"I did. I came to see Eel and wanted to talk to you. I can see you are busy. However, I do have a question for the doctor." He walked closer to the other man until he stood in front of him. "I think a short ride in a carriage might be the very thing to cheer the boy up."

Nicola jumped up. "I do not think—"

"I think, Mr. Barber, that might be a jolly good idea," the doctor interrupted. "I plan to come by in the morning, say eleven o'clock. Meet me then, and we can see how Eel is." He quieted Nicola's protest by touching her arm. "Children Eel's age and station in life can ill afford to lie about. Soon as the boy is over any real danger and feeling even a little better, he will want to be up."

"I do not want anything to happen to him. "

"Nicola." The doctor took hold of both her hands. "Nothing is going to happen to him. He needs to be careful for a fortnight. He will recover without any lasting injuries."

Clay watched this display, his stomach in a tight knot. His chest burned like it was on fire. He wanted to remove the doctor's hands from Miss Nicola, his Nicola.

Damn that woman.

He wished he could throw her over his shoulders and take her to his…

Time I went to visit Miss Lucille's house. I need some womanly companionship for an evening.

"Well, I will be leaving, Miss Highbridge, but I really do need to talk to you about George." He turned away and smiled to himself.

"Wait, what did you say?" Nicola pulled her hands away from the doctor and hurried toward him.

"I will come by this evening to discuss George and the museum unless you have a problem with that?"

"No but—"

"I will see you in the morning, doctor. Good afternoon." When he walked out, his mind should have focused on the darkened shadows across the street not on his Nicola and the doctor.

Chapter Eleven

"Regarding my appointment in the morning to see Eel," Peter said, as they walked into the foyer. "I will have to come later in the day. I have remembered a previous engagement." The doctor frowned and glanced toward the stairs. "May I see Eel again before I leave, to ensure he has recovered enough to be out and about tomorrow?"

"You will find me in the sitting room, first door on your right when you are back in the foyer." Nicola watched him hurry up the stairs.

Peter turned on the last step, smiled down at her, and disappeared from view.

Settling herself in the chair next to the piles of books scattered throughout the sitting room, Nicola leaned down, plucked the top book off the stack, and placed it in her lap.

Her main concern was for patients during the winter months. With despair she watched entire families fall seriously ill, older members dying from the start of one small cold.

The third time she read the same paragraph and could not remember a word she'd read, Nicola gave up. With her mind in such turmoil over the last few days, she hadn't opened a book, had hardly even glanced at one. Her mind was preoccupied with Mr. Barber, George, the follower, and then again Mr. Barber.

Gathering the books scattered about the room; some in precarious piles on the floor, others spread out on the table, she stacked them near the door, so they could be taken to her new study room.

It was all Mr. Barber's fault. Every time the man came into the room, her body temperature rose. She liked the way he looked—tall, rugged, and not too handsome. All she had to do was close her eyes to picture him dressed as a knight of yore. Her lips twitched. The opening of the door broke the spell.

"It appears Eel likes to sit in the chair watching the activity on the street," Peter said, as he walked into the room. "I think an outing tomorrow with Mr. Barber will be right for our brave lad."

"I think Eel should be ready to go home by the end of the week."

"It would be best to see how Eel manages an outing before we make a decision regarding his bed rest." Peter placed his hand on the back of her chair. "Again, thank you for the time you spent with me. I took great pleasure in my lesson and look forward to the next one."

"Might we discuss the time and content of your next lesson on your visit tomorrow? I must get this mess cleaned up now, or Aunt Belle will be very upset."

"I will be here very late in the day. It will depend on my earlier appointments."

Nicola stood. She wanted to get rid of the doctor so she could talk to Eel about George. She walked Peter to the door and quickly ran up the stairs, taking them two at a time. Not very lady-like, but then no one was watching. At least, not anyone she was aware of. The door to Eel's room stood open. She knocked and entered without waiting for an invitation. Eel sat paging through a picture book she'd left for him earlier in the day.

"How are you?"

"I be better and better." He pointed to the book. "I enjoy the pictures but can't wait until I can be reading the words."

"You will read sooner than you think, believe me." She pointed at him. "You are a very smart lad. I am off to see your mother for tea. But first I want to talk to you about George."

"What about 'im, miss?" The color disappeared from Eel's face.

"The word is, 'him' not ''im'." She listened as Eel repeated the word. "I noticed Mr. Barber has a great interest in George too. You seemed to know a great deal about him, even before the incident at the museum."

A scowl clouded Eel's face.

"You never explained why you were at the museum and why Mr. Barber came looking for you."

"Well, miss, you see Mr. Barber he be looking to find George. Mr. Barber…mmm…I be very tired." He snuggled under the covers and closed his eyes. "Could we be talking about this later?"

If he'd opened his eyes, he would have seen Nicola's smirk. It was obvious he didn't want to talk about Mr. Barber and George. She decided to give him time. Eel wouldn't be going far. People didn't keep information from her for very long, especially if she wanted to know something. She strolled over to the bed without making a sound and tucked him in, adding an extra quilt for warmth.

"You know, dear boy—" she bent down and whispered "—you and I will talk about George sooner or later."

****

Clay found Barnaby at the house pacing the floor.

"Where have you been?" Barnaby demanded, not giving him enough time to shut the door.

Clay didn't bother to answer. First, Barnaby wasn't his mother and secondly, he answered to no one. However, he had never seen Barnaby so agitated.

"I went to the hall of records looking for ownership of the building George disappeared into." Barnaby said, with a shrug of his shoulders. "Seemed like a right easy task. But the ownership is quite a maze and rather mysterious. An association owns the building and all the warehouses in the area, and continues to break into another group and another and another, and goes on and on." He put his hands on his hips and leaned against the kitchen sink. "The way I figure it, either someone or a group of individuals is trying real hard to hide the fact they're involved. Of course, the building could also be owned by somebody and leased to someone else." He sighed. "You do get where I be heading with this?"

"Yes. If someone important is trying to hide their involvement, it will not be easy to ferret him or her out. I think you should turn all this over to KM6." Clay removed his coat and hung it on one of the chair backs at the table. "They can list all the members of each association, and we will see who continues to show up over and over."

"I will need your written instructions." Barnaby handed Clay a cup of tea. "Don't give me your raised eyebrow looks. You know if I ask KM6 to do anything, they'll put it on the back shelf until they find the time. If you tell them in writing, it will be done in a matter of hours."

Three cups of tea with a touch of brandy later, both men were satisfied with their written request. It was simple and contained the date and enough information to aid in the search. Some pertinent information was omitted as one never knew when the wrong person might either hear or see the request. They made two copies, one for their records, which Barnaby kept hidden, and one for KM6.

Clay gave Barnaby a rundown on his day's activities. He failed to mention his increasing attraction to Nicola.

"I will be visiting Eel later and plan to speak to Miss Nicola," Clay said, and his voice softened as he said her name.

"Why do I think talking to that woman ain't going to be an easy task?" Barnaby chuckled.

"How right you are. For every question I ask, she is going to ask one in return, and I better have some answers. You and I have a strategy to plan." Clay closed his eyes, until Nicola's face filled his mind.

****

Nicola was busy checking her dried herb supply when the herbal room door opened.

"Good evening, Miss Highbridge. I hope I am not disturbing you…"

Nicola looked up but didn't say a word or smile.

"We do need to talk." He looked around the area. "I see your herbal study room has turned into an herbal practice. I'm not sure it's the wisest choice. I don't want to be overheard or interrupted so I took the liberty of locking the outside door." He didn't wait for her approval.

"Why are you here, Mr. Barber?" Before he could answer, she said, "Oh, yes, George."

Mr. Barber sat in the chair, his legs stretched out in front of him.

"I have to find a different table and chairs." She sat across from him.

"Why?"

"The small chairs and the table are too low to the ground for most men."

"A lot of men have been here today?" He shook his head. "I do not think—"

"A few Bow Street Runners and—"

"Miss Highbridge." Mr. Barber stood and looked down at her. "You should not be here by yourself with strange men. It is not safe."

"Mr. Barber"—she jumped to her feet—"do not tell me what to do. State the reason you have come or leave. I have much to do." She made a point of touching the piled herbs on the table.

"We need to talk about George and what happened at the museum," Clay said.

"First I want you to answer my questions. Why were you at the museum? Why is this George so important to you?"

Chapter Twelve

Inwardly, Clay smiled. He had planned for Nicola to react in this manner. His story was ready.

"I believe he knows who is responsible for my brother's death."

He hoped Nicola would accept the story as easily as Eel and didn't feel it necessary to mention the recent rumors of a conspiracy to kill cabinet members. The Spenceans had to be stopped at all costs. He didn't want to involve his Nicola. After all, she was a woman, albeit a wonderful one.

"Mr. Barber, I am truly sorry about your brother. There is more to your story, I am sure. You have deliberately left out information." She chewed on her lip.

"Miss Highbridge—" He cut himself short and ran his fingers through his hair. "This is absurd, you calling me Mr. Barber and me calling you Miss Highbridge. We have gone beyond those formalities. Please call me Clay and I will call you Nicola. I would like us to be friends."

I need the information she has and if she does not tell me…This woman is going to drive me to bedlam.

"If we are to be partners in locating George, I believe we should be on a first name basis too." Nicola smiled in her smug fashion, which meant trouble to Clay.

"Wait one moment. I never said anything about being partners. This could be dangerous, and you are a lady."

If I embarrass her, she might back down. I can hear Barnaby. 'Who are you kidding boy?' *But it is worth a try.*

"Those are my terms, you tell me everything, and only then will I tell you what I know. Otherwise, sir, there is the door." She pointed toward it.

He sat there stunned.

How did she do that? Turn everything around to her terms. Never in my lifetime has a woman ever turned the tables on me. Good thing Barnaby and I made up a story based more on fact.

"My friend and business partner Barnaby"—Clay began with a superior smirk—"has been looking for George with Eel's help, since before you came to London. That is why I met the mail coach. I hired Eel, and then he disappeared."

Nicola nodded.

"Eel discovered when George would be back in town. We tracked him from his rooms to the museum and planned to follow him when he left." He crossed his arms over his chest, scowled, and continued. "We were hoping it would reveal who he is working for outside the museum. When you and your sister arrived, we sent Eel to find out why you were there. I did not want George to become nervous and disappear. Which is what happened."

Nicola sat quiet for a long time.

"Well," he said, "now it's your turn to tell me what you know."

"I will be as honest with you as I think you are

being with me."

"Now wait one min—"

"Let me finish." She held up her hands to stop him. "George demanded my sister help him steal priceless artifacts from the museum. As young girls, my foster sisters, Mara, Emmy, and I formed a guild. Each of us has a special coin. If any member of the sisterhood has a problem and needs immediate help all she has to do is send her coin to another member. Emmy sent her coin to me and as you know Mara is already here." Taking the coin hung around her neck, she handed it to him.

"Did you feel that?" she whispered.

"Yes." He couldn't speak beyond the one word. The sensation he felt had gone straight to his loins. He wanted to grab her, make love to her right there on the table.

He shrugged away the thought and focused all his attention on what he held in his hand.

"This coin is very old. Roman, is it not?"

"Yes and it is why we named our guild 'The Sisterhood of the Coin.' We found the coins in an old Roman ruin near Bath when we were children. Each one has the owner's initial scratched into it." She took his warm hand and moved his index finger along the "N" on the reverse side of the coin. "Can you feel the letter?"

Pleasant tingling sensations continued to pass between them as their fingers touched. Neither wanted to be the first to release their hand from the gentle ribbon of vibration which coursed between them.

"If you ever need me send your coin and I will be there," he whispered, not wanting to break the spell.

She stared at him with such a wistful look in her

eyes it took all his willpower not to take her into his arms.

Their thoughts were interrupted when Emmy burst into the room.

"Nicola I need—oh, sorry. I did not know you were with someone." Emmy stood a few feet inside the door looking at them strangely.

Nicola sighed. "Come in, Emmy. We were discussing our friend George. We are quite finished.

"At least for the time being," Clay whispered so only Nicola could hear him. He stood. "It is time I take my leave. I have numerous errands to attend to." He touched Nicola's hand and again felt the tingling sensation. He squeezed her hand. "It is still there."

"Yes, it is." Nicola squeezed his hand back. "Fancy that."

"Did either of you say something?" Emmy asked.

"Nothing," Nicola said.

Emmy backed away and left as abruptly as she had arrived.

"Guess…mmm…Emmy left," Nicola said.

Clay walked around the table, took her in his arms, and kissed her. She kissed him back and snuggled into his arms. When he released her, they moved back to their original places, both grasping their chair backs.

"Who cares if she is gone?"

"I can see you are back to your normal self."

"What is that supposed to mean, miss?"

"You can be so nice and pleasant as long as you want information. Well, let me tell you, you do not know everything, Mr. Clay Barber." She whirled around and walked to the door, which led to the kitchen. "You can let yourself out," she shouted over her shoulder. "The door is behind you!"

He stood for a few minutes looking at the closed door.

That woman is going to be the death of me. When I think I have her right where I want her, she changes, for no reason at all.

He closed his eyes for a few minutes, then opened them.

What did she mean I do not know everything? She is keeping something from me. I *did not tell her everything, so I guess turnabout is fair play, even for a woman.* He shook his head and laughed as he walked out the door.

****

He should be thinking about finding his brother's killers, not thinking about Nicola Highbridge. Clay shook his head and ambled home. He hoped Barnaby would have more solid information to aid their search for the Spenceans. His residence in London was a poor excuse for living quarters. It was criminal anyone received rent money for a house in this condition. Yet it served his purpose to conceal his living in London. None of his acquaintances would dare be seen in this part of town.

Barnaby, for self-preservation, took over the duties of cooking. It was the only time Clay ate a decent home cooked meal. He was hungry and hoped Barnaby was home.

For once, something was going right with this mission. Yet, every time the pieces were falling into place someone—Nicola—got in the middle, stirred the pot and…Hell, he was tired of it all. Maybe it was time to get out of this game of intrigue.

Never before had Clay wanted to settle down and raise a family. Now he thought about it all the time. Clay Barber; agent, soldier, and peer, until now never staying in one place long enough to form any lasting relationships. True, the government always kept him on assignments and in truth he always liked the adventure, until now. Now he wanted Nicola and to make love to her every day for as long as they lived.

He would wager his prize horse that underneath those prim, proper clothes Nicola had a body made for loving. No, he should not be thinking about her like that. Nicola was a lady. He should go see Miss Lucille and get his basic needs taken care of. Hell, he wasn't interested in basic needs. It was Miss Nicola Highbridge who continued to fascinate him.

Barnaby met him at the door. "I could hear you stomping up the stairs. Just in time for dinner, as usual."

The smell of the stew and fresh bread wafted through the kitchen and encircled Clay.

"You, my friend, don't look so good. I take it your meeting did not go well."

"Had an interesting and very tiring conversation with that woman." Clay leaned against the kitchen table.

"Checking on the ownership of the building has given up some interesting information thus far." Barnaby rubbed his eyes and yawned.

"Pray tell. I am much too tired to guess." Clay for once managed to clear his thoughts of Nicola.

Barnaby set the food down in the center of the table.

"We can talk and eat." Clay sniffed the air. "I am

famished."

Both men attacked their evening meal of lamb stew, and bread still hot from the oven. After eating a large portion, Barnaby took his dishes to the sink to get them out of the way.

"I made a chart of sorts to keep track of the ownership, rents, and leases—very complicated business." Barnaby took a paper from his pocket and placed it on the far end of the table. He tried his best to smooth out the wrinkles on the large sheet. "There are two names in all the associations we have checked so far, Mr. Malcolm Lynford and a Mr. Shorts. I, with the help of KM6, am in the process of figuring out who and where they are. We still don't know who owns the property."

"The first name, Lynford, I have seen it before, or at least heard it, and not long ago, but where? Let me think while I finish eating."

Once again Clay's thoughts returned to Nicola. She had a quick mind, beautiful face, could talk about something other than marriage, children, and marriage. Why wasn't she married? He judged her to be four and twenty, maybe as much as eight and twenty. In most circles she would be considered on the shelf.

"Clay, I say, Clay."

His expression was blank when he looked over at Barnaby. "Sorry?"

"I know you have a lot on your mind." Barnaby put his hands in his pockets. "However National Security and our mission is—by the by how is our young lad doing? Tough for his age, ain't he?"

"Eel is fine." Clay raised his eyebrows. "Starting to feel better and wants back in the race to find George.

Figure he will be with us by Monday, if not sooner, if we can get him back home." Standing, Clay collected the dishes to take to the sink. "The Highbridge household keeps him in bed. Doctor Cooper is not helping matters. Looks to me like he's using Eel as an excuse to see more of Nicola."

"Oh, it's Nicola now. What happened to Miss Highbridge?" Barnaby shook his head. "By the by, you would not be jealous, would ya?"

"I think not."

A voice in his head whispered, "You would strangle the good doctor if you thought you could get away with it."

"You should see the look on your face." Barnaby chuckled. "It is a good thing the doctor is not here."

"The name, Malcolm Lynford, is…" Clay repeated as he walked around the table, stopped and leaned on its edge. "I can almost—"

Barnaby started cleaning up the kitchen.

Clay went to his jacket and retrieved an envelope from the inside pocket. "My father left this for me at headquarters with a note asking me to attend. I figured it to be another matchmaking effort by my parents. It is for a winter ball for February 10th, which is being given by a Malcolm Lynford. Do you think this could be the man listed in all the associations?"

"Don't know, but it is the best lead we have. I'll follow it up tomorrow. First thing," said Barnaby.

"And I will send an acceptance to Sir Malcolm Lynford's Winter Fantasy Ball. According to my father, it is the social event of the season.

Clay secretly looked forward to the first *Ton* affair he would attend in years. He would be able to spend some time with his parents and his friends. He was tired of hiding while in London. After the ball he might visit Miss Lucille's establishment.

Chapter Thirteen

A young boy, probably Eel's age, sat waiting with his grandmother when Nicola entered her herbal room from the kitchen hallway. She efficiently attended to the cut above his eye, scraped knuckles, and a swollen lip, while assuring the anxious woman he would heal in time. She confirmed a pregnancy for a young girl who was distraught. Unwed, she had no prospects of a husband. A second woman needed reassurance the life changes she was experiencing at her age were common, and there was no reason for alarm. She made special herbal tinctures for both women.

All of a sudden, it seemed the whole of London came marching to Nicola's doorstep, requiring some type of herbal care. Nicola would not turn anyone away. Everyone in the house offered to help. Her sisters went to the apothecary's shop for bottles and to the farmers' market for fresh herbs. The list was long, yet they managed to locate all the items. Cook and the maid cleaned bottles and jars. Sally patiently prepared herbs for tinctures and made garlands. Betsy cut bandages from Uncle William's old shirts.

If Nicola wasn't tending patients, she could be found concocting herbal remedies. She'd taken over a small section of the kitchen and part of the stove. Cook didn't object to her intrusion. However, at times the kitchen did become crowded.

Nicola at last went to see Eel after an early supper with the kitchen staff. When the rest of the Highbridge women ate later, she planned to be in bed sound asleep.

A writing lesson would give Eel something to do and keep him occupied while he convalesced, and it gave her an opportunity to discuss George. She lightly knocked on the door in case Eel was asleep. She was surprised when Jeb and Jimmy appeared and motioned her into the room.

Nicola walked over to the bed. "Did you enjoy your ride with Mr. Barber today?"

"It was grand, Miss. I sat up high and could see everyone and everything."

She decided a game was in order. The lads were far too serious. It would give them something to do, and she was interested in determining who was right-handed or left-handed. She tossed a ball to each boy to see which hand they used to catch it. Time and time again, Jeb used his left hand, while Jimmy and Eel their right hands.

Next, she conducted a test the gypsies used to determine which eye was dominant. Each lad raised one arm in front of him and pointed with his index finger to the portrait of Aunt Belle's great uncle, hanging above the fireplace. The lads pointed to his bulbous nose with both eyes opened. Then they closed one eye while still looking at the nose with their open eye. If their finger stayed pointed at the nose, in the same spot, when both eyes had been opened that was their dominant eye. If the finger pointed away from the spot then their other eye was dominant. This exercise determined which hand should be used doing tasks, which required the closing of one eye: shooting a gun or archery.

The game gave her a chance to watch and learn about each boy. She wasn't sure who laughed the hardest or the longest. There had been too little laugher in their short lives.

Eel and Jimmy were by far the quickest learners. Jeb was much slower but would surpass both Eel and Jimmy in his learning. It would simply take longer.

Jimmy would learn only because he saw the necessity in doing so, which meant he would only learn what he needed to get by.

Eel, on the other hand, wasn't as predictable. Nicola would hold her judgment until later.

She enjoyed the challenge of the three lads since there was never a dull moment when they were around. Nicola soon tired of Jeb's and Jimmy's numerous questions about the wonders and treasures they found in the room. She didn't think there was anything they hadn't touched or examined closely.

Leaving them to their laughter, she escaped to the peace and quiet of her herbal room.

****

Miss Nicola Highbridge was the real reason Clay once again ventured out on this cold and windy evening. His heart felt it, yet it had taken the entire walk for his brain to grasp the notion.

She had a way of sneaking into his thoughts. One minute he was thinking about his mission, finding the people responsible for his brother's death, then she appeared, and blocked out all else.

Clay took out his frustration on the door knocker and banged it hard three times.

"Good evening and who you be seeing, sir?" Sally asked.

"Miss Nicola and then Eel."

"Please to come into the warm sitting room."

He sat in a chair close to the fire and stretched out his hands. He'd once again forgotten his gloves, somewhere. He watched the flames flicker, and a small trail of smoke disappeared up the chimney. He looked around the room and noticed all the books were gone. He'd started to doze when the door opened.

"Mr. Barber, I see you are making yourself at home. I hope you are comfortable enough." Nicola stood a few feet from him.

"The fire feels wonderfully warm." He opened his eyes. "Would you care to join me?" He straightened himself in the chair, feasted his eyes on her, and motioned to his lap.

"You, sir, are the most..." Sighing, she shook her head.

"Haven't thought of a word for me yet, I take it. You will soon enough, I'm sure." He laughed.

"Why are you here?"

He reached for her hand. She quickly put her hands behind her back.

"I thought we agreed it would be Clay and Nicola."

"That was then, this is now."

He walked over to Nicola and studied her face for a few seconds. He moved closer and closer. When he was inches from her, he reached out and wrapped his arms around her and kissed her inviting lips. He didn't wait for a reaction but deepened his kiss. Their bodies molded together, and her arms encircled him.

Clay, feeling a sudden rush of pleasure, pushed his body backward. Nicola stood still. Her arms floated to her side as she frowned. At that moment he realized how unique she was.

She does not try to be what I want her to be. She is what she wants to be, and independent in the process.

He has been looking for a woman like Miss Highbridge his entire adult life

Nicola stirred and managed to push away from him. Her hand brushed across her lips. Her tongue followed the path of her hands. Nicola's lips felt so alive, on fire, and yet cool to her touch. She stared at Clay as she felt a stirring deep in her body. When she tried to pinpoint where, she couldn't. First, it flashed hot and then just a steady pulsing that all but disappeared. However, a feeling of need remained. She floated to the fireplace with her back to him. She couldn't face him until she composed herself.

Aunt Belle, Emmy, and Mara paraded single file into the room, stopping inside the door.

"Good evening, Mr. Barber. Will you be joining us for tea?" Aunt Belle moved toward her favorite overstuffed green chair.

"I came to call on Eel. We have some business to discuss."

"Well, go visit our brave lad, and then please join us, Mr. Barber," Emmy said.

"Yes, please do." Mara handed him a glass of brandy from the sideboard. "I thought you might like this. You seem to be off thinking about something."

"It seems all I do is fantasize about a certain someone," Clay whispered.

Mara smiled. "I noticed."

Draining the glass with one gulp, he moved across the room and sat it on the empty tray sitting on the sideboard. "Nicola, please come with me. I have something to discuss with you and Eel."

"I do not think…"

"Dear gel, that is fine." Aunt Belle opened her fan. "Come back promptly in twenty minutes. Will that give you enough time to see our brave lad, Mr. Barber?"

"Yes ma'am," Clay replied.

He reached for Nicola's hand the moment the door closed behind them. She started to pull away and then settled her fingers into his. A ribbon of energy coursed between them. She liked the feel of his strong grip as well as the man.

The boys were still visiting Eel; their laughter could be heard as the couple approached the room.

"We came to discuss George and friends," Clay said, as they entered.

"About time," she muttered.

Clay scowled at her and explained the difficult process of determining ownership of the building George had disappeared into. He recruited Jimmy and Jeb's help for the following day.

"What about me?"

"Eel, you are not well enough," Nicola said.

"I-I—" the boy stammered.

"Listen to me." She touched Eel's arm. "You are important to all of us. You must do as you are told or you might never become strong again."

"You must follow Miss Nicola and the doctor's instructions to the letter." Clay turned and caught the smell of the still air in the closed up sick room and the odor of stale food.

"Only sissies stay in bed and I ain't no sissy and—"

"Oh, you think so." Clay scowled. "Well, let me

tell you a thing or two." He put his hands up to stop Eel when he tried to talk. "When I was a few years older than you, I fell off my horse and badly injured my leg. At first, I was having too much discomfort to care about being stuck in bed. As I got better, I tried to make everyone else as miserable as I felt. I carried on and complained until everyone gave in and let me do what I wanted. The first day I hobbled around, the second day I fell down the stairs, hurt my back, arm, and reinjured my leg. So instead of being in bed for two weeks I spent two whole months there. Believe me, after that I stayed in bed until the doctor said I could leave." He pointed to Nicola. "You do what Miss Nicola tells you, or you will not be working for me, now or ever."

"It ain't fair, sir." Eel stared hard at Clay. "You have all the excitement while I be stuck 'ere in this old bed."

"It will only be for a couple more days. I promise we will be sure to save some excitement for you." Nicola said.

Betsy came into the room with a tray piled high with biscuits, small pink and white frosted cakes, tea, and hot chocolate.

The smells of the hot chocolate and food caught Jimmy and Jeb's attention. The eager look on their faces was a sure sign there wouldn't be a crumb left.

Nicola enlisted Clay's help with the arrangement of a small ornate table next to Eel's bed so the boys could talk while they ate.

"My lady, it is time for our tea. Please come with me," Clay announced, taking her hand and bowing. He winked at the boys who were watching his every move as he and Nicola walked out the door.

He stopped halfway down the hallway and took her in his arms and kissed her. When he tried to pull away, she wrapped her arms around him, and held him close.

"You must let me go, or I will take you into one of the bedrooms and not let you out until morning."

She dropped her arms, looked up at him as she moved toward the stairs.

"Wait," Clay said.

"When you take me in your arms I get so confused." She ran her tongue over her pulsing lips. "It feels so right, but it is so wrong. Is it not?"

"It is not inappropriate, believe me, my dear. I am becoming quite attached to you and holding you in my arms is what comes of my feelings for you. You care about me too. I know you do. Am I right?" he asked.

"You are not part of my plans," she said. "I cannot and will not be attracted to you."

"Plans, what plans? I am talking about—"

"Oh, there you are," Mara said, the moment she entered the hallway from the stairs. "Aunt Belle sent me to fetch the two of you. Tea is being served in the green sitting room, and you do not want to be late."

"Why do you say green sitting room? I hate to bring this up, but everything in this house is green. Am I the only one who has noticed?" Clay rubbed the side of his face.

"Yes, Mr. Barber, we noticed. How could we not? It is Aunt Belle's new favorite color. You should have been here when her favorite color was pink." Mara laughed.

Nicola groaned. "I hate to imagine it."

The two women walked down the stairs, arm in arm, in front of Clay. He tried to think of an excuse to leave. He didn't know if he could sit through tea and chit-chat. Too many things on his mind.

Following the two women into the sitting room, he found the only available seat was next to Nicola. The minute he sat next to her, he reached for her hand. The tingling sensation, again, passed between them.

Sally entered the sitting room after knocking three times. "Miss Nicola, two men be in the sick room."

Chapter Fourteen

Nicola was happy for an excuse to be away from Clay and made for the door. But she found him right behind her. "What are you doing?" she demanded

"I am coming with you. You do not know who these men are."

"Mr. Barber, how very kind." Aunt Belle pursed her lips. "I do worry about some of the ruffians who have paid a visit to Nicola's herbal room. Please take him with you, my dear."

"Aunt Belle, these men are…"

Shaking her head with disgust, Nicola left the room. She stopped as Clay shut the door behind them.

"You are not to interfere with my work. Do you understand me?"

"Yes ma'am." Clay bowed. "I will just be your protector." Taking her hand, he squeezed and kissed her fingertips.

Now he is acting like my knight in shining armor.

A rush of warmth spread through her entire body, leaving in its wake a need she had never experienced before. Oh Lord, she wanted to rush into his arms and…

"Nicola, earlier you spoke of plans. What plans?" He followed her into the kitchen.

"You be needing more hot water, miss?" Cook asked, as Nicola picked up the pot from the stove.

"At this point I am not sure. Please put another pot on. If I need it, Mr. Barber can fetch it."

They walked into the herbal room and found two men at the table drinking tea from dainty china cups.

"What have we here?" Nicola asked.

One man's leg was encased in a blood-soaked cloth. His arm was laced with superficial cuts. One eye was half-closed and had already turned black and blue.

"There were a fight over on Humboldt Street, and I were right in the middle of it. I be from Bow Street, miss." He motioned to the other man standing against the wall. "Jake here said I should come."

"Let me look at your leg and decide if I can help. You have to remove your pants or I can cut them. Your choice." She put two drops of poppy juice in a large glass, then added hot water and enough cold water so he could drink it. "If it is cool enough, drink it all now. It will help to dull the pain."

She went to the cabinet and took out a small leather case, which contained packets of dried herbs. She steeped the herbs in hot water to make a healing compress to cover the wounds.

"Your name is?"

"Smithy." When she raised her eyebrows, he continued. "I were a smith before I come to Bow Street. Don't practice the trade now, but the name stuck."

"This is going to hurt some, Smithy, but it cannot be helped. The wound must be cleaned or it will become infected."

"I understands, miss. You best get to it."

"Clay, would you take Jake to the kitchen for some tea until we are done."

"I be willing to hold him down, miss. If need be."

117

Jake walked toward the injured man.

'That is up to Smithy."

"Jake, you go with the gentleman."

"We be close by miss," Jake said. "If you need help, call out. We'll step outside for some fresh air."

When the men left, a cool breeze wafted into the room. The air mixed with the herbs and spread their fragrance into the space.

"It would be easier for both of us if you could move to the table against the wall. You will be more comfortable." Nicola walked over, pulled down the two lanterns above the table, lit them, and pushed them back in place. They gave off the right amount of light for her to stitch up his leg.

Smithy hobbled over to the table and lay down. Nicola took a deep breath and started work; the cut was deep but not long. It did however, expose muscle and bone. She cleaned it with lavender, black walnut hulls, and St. John's wort. At the last minute, she added elderflower for its antifungal properties. It took fifty stitches to close up the wound. She put the herbal compress over it and bandaged his leg with clean soft cloths. Nicola sewed up his pants leg as best she could. Smithy said not a word, although sweat beaded around his forehead. She poured him a drink of Irish whiskey she kept for such occasions.

When she finished, Nicola sat in the chair to catch her breath. Her concentration was so intense when she worked, she lost track of time.

"It appears you be done?"

"Except for a few instructions. Can you sit up and walk back to the chair to make sure your leg can handle the movement. I shall tidy up while you catch your breath."

She put all the bloody towels in a bucket and poured hot water over them until they were completely covered. She put the herbs back in the pantry. Dried herbs needed to be kept in a darkened place so they wouldn't lose their curative power. She couldn't resist standing in front of the pantry door and taking a few deep breaths.

It continued to amaze her that the thought of the patient's problem produced the name of the herb she needed. She smiled and a calmness came over her. Some might call it her intuition. She preferred to think the gypsy way—her healing power sought knowledge from the plants. All conversation stopped when she and Smithy walked into the kitchen.

"Your friend should take it easy for the next couple of weeks," she said, looking at Jake. "He needs to come back to have the stitches taken out in ten days."

"I can take out them stitches for Smithy, miss."

"I am sure you could, Jake. But there is a possibility the stitches might have to stay in longer. It depends on how the wound heals, and I need to check for infection. However, it would be helpful if you could change the bandages every day."

"I can do me own changing," Smithy said.

"I am sure you could," Nicola said. "But it would be easier for someone else to do it. Believe me, it is hard to a do a proper job. If Jake cannot manage, come here, and I will."

"Tea. Sit and drink it." Clay set cups in front of Nicola and Smithy.

They drank their tea and talked of the weather, the crazy king, and the regent. When the men announced they were leaving to report back to Bow Street. Clay left with them.

The moment she was alone, weariness settled over her. She swept the healing room and made sure everything was in its proper place. Tomorrow was another day.

She used her homemade herbal soap to wash out the bloody towels. Nicola left them soaking in clean hot water and tomorrow Betsy would wash them again so they could be reused. She scrubbed the tabletop, sat down, and put her head in her hands.

Nicola closed her eyes and in slow motion, played the scene in the sitting room with Clay over and over in her mind. Her lips felt so alive, on fire, and yet cool to the touch. She had felt a stirring deep in her body. When she tried to pinpoint where, she couldn't. First, it flashed hot and then followed a steady pulsing that all but disappeared. However, a feeling of need remained. Her mind continued to whirl around her feelings for Clay. Why wasn't she able to think of anything else?

She stood up, took one last look around the room, locked up, and went upstairs.

****

Eel hadn't told anyone about his sleepless nights. He couldn't always remember the details, only the evil waiting out of reach, lurking in the shadows. He was still awake when the clock struck midnight. It seemed senseless to lie in bed another moment, so he dressed as quickly as he could and hurried to the shed behind the dress shop. He needed to talk to Jimmy and Jeb.

The shed was cold, drafty, and dreary. The paint had long ago peeled leaving the wood exposed. Yet, Jimmy and Jeb called it home. It wasn't much, but it was better than living on the streets, especially in the winter. It contained a few pieces of cast off furniture, a table with a broken leg, and an old bed frame with a straw filled mattress, an assortment of bedding, an old wood stove, and two chairs. In the corner sat a wooden crate full of clothing.

Eel lit a small candle in a broken dish near the center of the table. He pulled up one of the rickety chairs and collapsed onto it. He couldn't stand or walk any further. He rested his elbows on the table. The cold had snuffed out the little energy he had. His mates had probably found a warmer place to stay the night.

Why had he not listened to Mr. Barber and Miss Nicola?

He'd felt fine in the nice soft bed and enjoyed having an aunt, even if it was in name only. After his heroic act, she insisted he call her Aunt Belle. He put his head on the table to rest. The creaking door woke him. He looked up and was surprised to see Clay glowering at him.

"What are you doing here, boy?"

Eel rubbed his eyes.

"Well, answer me."

"I be sitting here waiting for Jimmy and Jeb." He leaned into the table, letting his head sit in the palm of his hand.

"Why?"

"Something be wrong." Eel closed his eyes and kept them closed. "There be evil about so I be 'ere, here, to talk to me mates." Eel opened his eyes and squinted as the guttering candle offered little light.

"I, too, want to talk to your friends." Clay moved closer. "You need to be back in bed. I'll take you to

Miss Nicola. On the way, we can discuss this evil you think is about."

Eel tried to stand but found he had no energy to move. Clay caught the boy before he hit the dirt floor, scooped him up, and made for the door. But then he remembered the burning candle and turned back. The last flicker of flame turned to a small sliver of smoke, and they silently left the shack.

Barnaby was so tired if he leaned against the shop wall he might fall asleep. He continued to scan the street looking for someone or something out of place. Clay crept up behind his friend and stayed far enough back to be hidden if someone was watching.

"What have you there?" Barnaby spoke barely moving his lips.

"A young lad who is not as well as he thought." Clay tried to protect Eel from the wind. "Can you find a carriage and meet me at the entrance to the mews?"

"Will do. I have not seen anything or anyone out of the ordinary."

"Good," Clay turned, shifted his bundle, and moved to the back gate, which led into the mews. The carriage stopped at the street. Barnaby jumped down, opened the door, and helped Clay with the boy.

Eel stirred. "My eyes will not stay open."

"You have more nerve than sense, boy."

"Yes, he does. I, for one, am glad he is on our side." Barnaby touched the boy's arm.

"I do not want to wake anyone when we get to the Highbridge house." Clay shifted his stance.

"No problem." Barnaby patted his breast pocket where he kept his lock picks. "You and the boy wait in the carriage. I will whistle when the door is open." He hit the top of the carriage and called out to the driver. "Pull around the corner mate."

Barnaby moved into the yard but stayed concealed in the darkened shadows. His gloved hand reached out to touch the library door handle, but froze in place.

The door had been left open, not much, but enough for a small piece of drapery to be caught in the opening. He peered into the room before stepping into the deeper shadows away from the door. He ran back the way he had come.

At the sound of approaching footsteps, Clay laid Eel on the seat of the carriage, covered him with his coat, and jumped out. Barnaby grabbed the door to keep it from slamming and moved toward Clay.

"The door was open," Barnaby whispered. "I could see shadows of people, holding candles, moving in the library, and the hall beyond. I guess there be two to three men." He caught his breath and added, "Too large to be any of the women."

"Damn, damn." Clay muttered under his breath. "We have to move now! She is in danger again!"

"What about Eel?" Barnaby opened the carriage door. "We cannot carry him about and do what needs to be done."

"We will take him with us," Clay said. "We can lay him on the couch or the floor in the library, out of harm's way."

The moon hid behind the clouds as Barnaby paid the driver. Clay jumped into the carriage, causing it to rock from side to side, and handed the sleeping boy down to Barnaby's waiting arms.

They wove their way through the grounds and drifted into the library. Barnaby laid Eel on the small love seat and covered him with their coats. Eel flinched.

"You stay here. Do not make a sound," Barnaby whispered and put the tips of his fingers on Eel's lips.

Eel nodded his head.

Clay and Barnaby heard voices coming from the hallway. The sounds of their voices gave the direction they appeared to be traveling. One voice receded toward the back of the house and one faded going up the staircase. A third man lurked in the shadows of the small alcove in the hallway.

The men retraced their steps through the library and stayed in the shadows around the side of the house. Barnaby, a master at picking locks, had the door of the herbal room open in less time than it took to say the king was mad.

Once inside, they had reached the kitchen door when they heard approaching footsteps. Clay positioned himself on one side of the door while Barnaby took the other. When it opened, Clay spun the intruder around. Barnaby landed a solid facer, knocking him out cold. Clay found rope and tied him up, while Barnaby stuffed a roll of bandages in his mouth.

They ran through the kitchen and into the front hallway where the smell of cheap liquor floated from the alcove. Barnaby reached in and bashed the guard over the head with a blackjack. The man slept on. Clay tied him up and dumped him into a closet off the hallway.

The men scrambled up the stairs. When they entered the corridor, they paused long enough to let their eyes adjust to the darkness. A faint light shone beneath a doorway at the far end of the hallway. The men rushed toward it, listening for sounds of a struggle.

They were almost there when another door ahead flew open.

A dark figure raced out with Nicola closely behind, a candlestick in one hand and a gun in the other.

"You wretched, vile, dirty excuse, of a—" Nicola shouted, advancing toward the man who retreated to the top step.

"Please allow me." Clay grabbed Nicola around the waist and pushed her behind Barnaby and himself. He snatched the gun from her hand.

Both men advanced toward the intruder who ran down the staircase, but tripped, balancing first on one foot, then the other. Then losing complete control, he somersaulted to land in a heap at the bottom.

Peering into the foyer's darkness, Clay, Barnaby, and Nicola stood in silence. The figure lying on the floor didn't budge. Before anyone could utter a word, Aunt Belle, Susan, and Emmy filled the air with excited chatter, everyone asking questions at the same time.

Nicola took the single candle Emmy held and, being very careful, moved downstairs. Clay and Barnaby followed close behind. Holding the candle high, she looked first in Clay and Barnaby's direction.

"You both have some explaining to do." She pushed her hair away from her face. "Do not give me that look, Mr. Barber, or you either."

She peered at the man with Clay and asked, "Who are you?"

"Barnaby, miss." He walked away.

"You two are not to leave until I have some answers." She tapped Clay's arm.

Chapter Fifteen

"My dear"—Clay tried to take Nicola's hand, but she pulled it out of his reach—"we will answer all your questions." He turned to Barnaby. "Go fetch the Bow Street Runners."

Nicole hurried over to Eel, who sat on the floor near the library door. He held a large walking stick in his hands.

"What did you think you were going to do with that?" She grabbed the stick and gave it to Emmy. "Young man, you are supposed to be in your bed, which I believe is upstairs."

"Yes, but when I heard the noise I be finding the biggest object I could." He pointed to the umbrella rack by the door. "To protect you."

"I am sure you have a good reason for being dressed and downstairs in the hallway. I cannot wait to hear it." She took his hand and squeezed it. "You stay right here."

She peered at the unconscious man at the bottom of the stairs. She should see to his injuries or should she leave him? Well she could, but no, she wouldn't.

As she approached the intruder, Clay pulled her back.

"Do not touch him. He could be faking his injuries."

"I am a healer." She drew her robe tighter. "I

would not want him to suffer needlessly because I sat and did nothing."

"Let us get some proper light so you can see."

Clay directed everyone to gather all the candlepower they could carry. With the hallway all aglow, Nicola convinced everyone except Clay to go into the sitting room.

Mara, the ever proper hostess, finally awakened by the commotion, quickly instructed Cook to prepare tea.

Clay carried Eel back into the library and gave him strict instructions not to move from the love seat where he carefully laid him down. Aunt Belle found a blanket and covered the boy, tucking it around the edges so only his face was uncovered.

Clay walked around the body and kicked the sole of the intruder's shoe to see if he stirred. There was no response, not even a twitch. He touched the man's leg with the toes of his boot.

Reaching down, too fast for Clay to stop her, Nicola felt for a pulse on the intruder's neck. "Turn him over," she said. "I believe our uninvited guest is dead."

"I do not think you should be a witness to such a dreadful event," Clay said.

"Event?" Her eyebrows shot up, and she sighed.

He shook his head, grimacing.

"You are impossible, Mr. Barber. Please turn him over now." She stood straight and marched toward Clay. "Now."

In the process of turning over the intruder, his knitted cap fell off, revealing long flowing red hair. Nicola looked closer at the face and noticed fine traces of face powder.

"Our intruder is a she and is dead." Nicola leaned

down and gently closed the intruder's unseeing eyes.

"I can see the facial features look feminine. Are you sure?" Clay moved closer to Nicola. "But—"

"Turn your back and I will check further."

"She is dead. What difference will it make?" Clay touched Nicola. She again felt the pulsing current until he removed his hand.

"Respect is given in life and death, no matter the person. Turn around."

Clay obeyed with a flourishing bow.

She found breast bindings. The woman had gone to a great deal of trouble and discomfort to hide her gender.

"You may turn around. It is a woman." Nicola finished buttoning up the intruder's shirt.

Curious about the cause of death, she looked closer and discovered a bloody knife handle sticking out of the woman's clothing. She grasped the knife and pulled with all her strength and staggered backward when the knife pulled free. Taking small scissors, from her pocket, she cut away some of the woman's bloody clothing to reveal numerous deep and ragged knife wounds.

Nicola pictured the woman with the drawn knife she chased out of her bedroom and into the hallway. The knife and the woman rolled down the stairs together, and at each turn the knife must have entered the intruder's body. She winced at the pain the woman must have felt.

Nicola would like to have seen the unclothed body to determine the exact cause of death, but she didn't think that would be possible, not in London.

Over the years she'd developed a keen interest in

such matters, honed her skills at determining cause of death, and the difference between murder and natural deaths. Constables in many local towns near her home enlisted her help from time to time.

Barnaby and two Bow Street Runners entered the house as noisy as a troop of soldiers. They stopped to look at the dead body. Nicola explained her discovery and covered the woman with a blanket Mara handed her.

But when they proceeded first to the closet, and then the healing room, they found the captives gone.

A chill ran up Nicola's back at the thought that in all the confusion, someone had entered, released the intruders, and disappeared.

The men searched the entire house from top to bottom with the exception of Aunt Belle's room, which was left to Nicola and Mara. Aunt Belle insisted no man enter her room under any circumstances.

On the back stairs, Nicola found a silver button. It was polished, very high quality, and unique in design. A silver portion was inlaid into a carved piece of bone. An ugly dog's head decorated the face. A peculiar design formed the dog's collar. At one time, it might have spelled a name, but it was too worn to read.

Nicola returned downstairs to discover Clay, Barnaby, and the body of the intruder gone. In the kitchen stood two Runners she didn't recognize.

"Miss, we been instructed to watch over the 'ouse for the remainder of the night," said the taller of the two men.

"We be hidden out of sight. You and your family will be safe," said the second man with a toothless grin.

Before she could formulate any questions, the men

vanished into the night.

"Eel is back in bed and sound asleep, Emmy as well, and of course Aunt Belle." Mara approached her at the foot of the stairs. "I am afraid, your interrogation of Eel will have to wait until morning."

Too exhausted to think any further about the night's problems, Nicola climbed the stairs, went to bed, and fell into an exhausted sleep.

****

Early the next morning, Nicola opened her eyes and found Eel's warm brown eyes staring directly into hers. Their faces were mere inches apart.

"Miss Nicola, miss, I remembers where I seen the woman who fell down them stairs."

"What did you say?" She yawned as she struggled to untangle herself from the covers, and finally managed to pull herself into a sitting position.

Eel shivered and hugged his arms around himself. The oversized robe he'd managed to find did little to keep him warm. She lifted blankets and motioned for him to climb into the warm bed.

"Oh, miss, it ain't proper," His teeth began to chatter.

"You are a child and cold." She tried not to look too stern.

She got out of bed, stirred the fire, added some coals, and scampered back under the warm covers.

"Now, Eel, where did you say you saw the dead lady?"

"The day we went to the store for my school books. Her were shopping too. And the day Jimmy and Jeb went with us. I think they seen her."

"I wonder—"

The door burst open.

"Wait until you see what I have," Mara waved a snow-white envelope over her head as she danced in place. She paced back and forth. Eel and Nicola's laughter stopped her in her tracks.

"Sit down," Nicola said. "You are wearing me out."

"I am sorry. I do my best thinking when I'm in motion." Mara settled her shawl around her shoulders and collapsed in the chair next to the bed.

"What is there to think about?" Nicola arranged the pillow behind her.

"An invitation for the Highbridge women and Aunt Belle to the ball of the season. Can you see us all dressed up?" Mara jumped to her feet and twirled around. "Our card full of dance partners. We shall be the belles of the ball."

"Consider first, I have no fancy dresses and no desire to attend a ball." Nicola punched the pillows in an attempt to make herself more comfortable. "Why, pray tell, is this invitation so important?"

"Well, it is from Lord Malcolm Lynford," Mara announced in a haughty tone and placed both hands on her hips. "His Winter Fantasy Ball is the most sought after invitation, the major event of the year, and is over the top." Fanning herself with the invitation, she continued, "Everyone who is anyone is invited, even the Prince Regent. In the years I have lived with Aunt Belle we have never, I repeat never, ever been invited. One of his many mistresses is one of my best customers and—what is Eel doing in your bed?

"He had a bad dream and came in here." Nicola winked at Eel and smiled at Mara. "The fire was just embers and the room very cold. So here we are."

"Fine, fine. You know we have talked for days about your lack of proper dress. Now, we will have to gather you a new wardrobe," Mara announced.

"I like my clothes, they are—"

"Really?" Mara sighed, as she walked over to the wardrobe and opened the door and removed one of her sister's dresses. "Well, living in a backwater town kept you from not only the latest fashions, but any fashion, I dare say."

"I know, Mara. I leave my wardrobe, or lack of, in your capable hands." She suppressed a laugh because for once Mara was going to do what she wanted her to do. In fact this would be a first; Mara was going to plan her new wardrobe.

"Eel and I have errands to run."

"I will bring some fashion plates home later and some material so we can begin."

"Eel." Nicola studied the boy for a few minutes. "You need to explain why you were dressed and downstairs last night."

"I could not sleep. Went downstairs when I heard the noise."

"Starting today, I want you to be up and about more, and for longer periods of time. You will get your strength back sooner. Get dressed, and I shall meet you downstairs for breakfast.

Eel slipped out of bed. The huge robe billowed out behind him, dusting the floor as he hurried to his room.

"Nicola, put on your chemise. I will get my measuring tape." Mara pointed a finger at her. "Do not give me that look of yours. It will only take a few minutes."

Nicola paused to remember a time when Mara manipulated her and Emmy to be her unwilling models, and it didn't appear much had changed. Mara was as bossy as ever when she wanted something.

Nicola's measurements were completed in less than ten minutes. It was easy to let Mara have her way. Her sister started out the door still mumbling about this dress, that dress, and a myriad of colors.

Nicola called after her. "Please keep them simple, and no pastels, please."

Mara backed up a few steps, and looked at her sister. "Oh, Nicola, trust me, I have the very thing."

By the time Nicola reached the kitchen, Eel had breakfasted and left for the healing room. She ate two warm scones dripping in honey, all the more enjoyable for the wonderful smells of food wafting around. After washing her hands, she went to the healing room, which to her surprise was full of people.

There goes my talk with Eel. I am not sure I believe his reason for being downstairs. And I bet Mr. Barber is involved.

Eel organized the patients, putting the most injured or sickest first. She stood and listened while he gave out orders. It surprised her that the adults listened to a child, but then Eel wasn't the average child. He was, she thought, an adult who happened to look like a child.

It took most of the morning and into the afternoon before she finished. There had been a painful burn, two broken fingers, and a nasty cut, which required stitches, another young woman too young to be having a babe and many, many more, minor complaints.

Her mind continued to be occupied with Clay whenever she let down her guard. She was disappointed he had not shown up to discuss the intruders or offer any information about the dead woman.

"I am off to complete my errands," she announced, as the last patient walked out.

"I would like to go with you, miss."

"I could wait until you take a nap." She bit the inside of her lip to keep from smiling as she waited for Eel's reaction.

"I not be a baby. I can—"

"You either take a short nap or I will leave without you." She stood and started to walk toward her cape hanging on the peg near the door.

"You promise not to be leavin' without me?" Eel hung his head.

"I promise. Off you go. I will be up to tuck you in soon."

By the time she got to the boy's room, he was fast asleep. Nicola sat in a chair next to his bed reading a herbal book while she waited for him to wake up.

Eel was awake in two hours and ready to leave the house within minutes. With the intruder's button in the pocket of the new navy-blue Spencer jacket Mara had given her, they left. She and Eel were going on a treasure hunt to look for the owner of the button.

One of her patients, this very morning, had told her of a shop, which had all manner of buttons. The shop made a majority of their own fasteners but did purchase a few specialty items. The establishment, Bailes Buttons, would be their first stop.

Nicola shuddered at the sight of the shop; it looked neglected and forlorn. No light showed through the store front windows. She peered in and observed a curtain covered in fine layers of dust, cobwebs, and attached to one side of the wall. Nicola turned the door handle and as inconspicuously as she could, entered the shop, which was very quiet. A narrow pathway wound through the boxes of buttons sitting precariously on the floor and on narrow crooked shelves. Glass jars, full of buttons covered in grime, stood at attention along the counter that ran the length of the room.

As Eel shut the door behind them, a box of buttons crashed to the floor. The noise of the wooden container disintegrating on impact startled both Eel and Nicola. They stood and watched the contents in slow motion scatter far and wide.

"Not to worry about them there buttons. We'll find them when we need them." An old man appeared in a curtained doorway at the back of the shop. "It weren't your fault they fell." He walked over to a high stool behind the counter and sat down.

A younger man appeared next and guided them to the center of the counter. Unshaven and dressed in wrinkled clothes, he took a large push broom and started to shove the mess of loose buttons under the closest table. A cloud of dust followed each movement. A damp and musty smell filled the air. With the toe of his shoe, he pushed a single fastener the broom missed under another table. Picking up the broken wooden box, he returned to the back of the store and disappeared. A fine cover of dust settled back in place once the curtain stopped moving.

Nicola placed the dog button in the old man's outstretched hand. He examined it and then took a small knife and poked it.

"Where did you find such an interesting bone button?"

"At my aunt's home." She reached out and retrieved the button from the man's hand.

"Why do you want more of these? I have much finer buttons or fasteners than the likes of this."

"I am trying to locate its owner. It appears to be special. I hoped you might know whom it belonged to."

"I cannot help you," he said a little too quickly. "I am not familiar with the style. My shop would never have sold anything this crude. For a price I could try and locate the owner for you."

Nicola had no hesitation in refusing the offer. She had seen similar buttons near the front door as she entered. So she thanked the man and left with hers safely tucked into her jacket pocket.

Just beyond the shop, a young girl reached out and grabbed Eel's arm. He drew back his fist until he saw the head of heavy black curls.

Chapter Sixteen

"Janey Ann, why you do that?" Eel shouted.

"Needs to tell you somethin'."

"Why not call out to me? Why you be 'iding?"

"A man." Janey Ann said, pointing to the back of the building. "He be watchin' you. Asks me who you be and all." The little girl scratched her head. "I not tell him nuffin', I runned away."

"Can you describe him?" Nicola asked.

"Who be her?" The child asked, narrowing her eyes as she moved closer to Eel.

"My friend," Eel said, taking Nicola's hand. "Miss Nicola, this 'ere be Janey Ann Jakes," said Eel. "Her also be a friend."

"I thinks it best if we be leavin'. Right now," Janey Ann said.

"Excellent idea. Come with us. We will go to my aunt's and have our afternoon tea."

She kept hold of the little girl's hand while the three of them hurried to the carriage parked down the street. Returning to the house, Nicola and Eel settled Janey Ann at the table in the sitting room. They loaded it with food and hot tea.

Nicola and Eel sat down to discuss their afternoon outing, until Mara came swirling in with an armful of boxes. Jeb and Jimmy followed close behind, their arms filled with packages. Each box had a colored ribbon holding it closed. Mara dropped the boxes at her feet and took a deep breath.

"These contain a small portion of your new wardrobe, Sister Dear."

"You cannot mean all this is for me?" Nicola picked up a small box.

Every time my sisters call me Sister Dear they are up to something.

"Oh yes, look." Grabbing the package from Nicola's hand, Mara opened the box and pulled out a pair of soft, white kid gloves. The next box she opened, she paused and smiled. "Cannot be showing unmentionables in mixed company—no matter the lads' ages." Moving on to a larger box, she pulled out a beautiful, aubergine dress with gold braid trim.

"Is this for me?" Nicola lightly touched the fabric.

"Some might say you should be wearing white since you have not had a coming out season. But at your age you would look ridiculous."

"I trust your judgment."

"Let me show you all the articles upstairs in your room. Eel, Jimmy, and Jeb, take the packages and follow me," Mara said.

Parading behind her, they filled their arms with packages and dumped them on the bed in Nicola's room. Some slid to' the floor under the bed and were retrieved by one of the lads. Nicola made to leave surrounded by the boys.

"Where do you think you are going?" Mara asked, one eyebrow arched.

"Remember—reading, writing, and arithmetic?" Nicola said.

"Oh, I forgot. I did wonder why the lads were here

when I drove up. Could you start a few minutes late so I can show you the dresses?"

"We be going to check on Janey Ann and will wait in the healing room for you, miss," Eel said.

"Thank you." Nicola smiled. "Ask Cook to give some cakes to Janey Ann and please see she gets home. Your lessons will start as soon as you get back."

"Oh, Miss Nicola."

She looked at Jimmy and Jeb standing next to Eel.

"I…" Jeb continued after Jimmy jabbed him in the ribs. "I told two others about the lessons. They wants to learn too." He took a deep breath. "I told 'em they be 'aving to ask you." He sighed. "I thinks they be 'ere."

"That should be fine." Nicola smiled. This was the most she'd ever heard him say. "Ask them to wait. I will be there in a few minutes."

Mara tore open the largest boxes. Nicola couldn't believe all the beautiful dresses. There were six in all and each prettier than the last.

"These are day gowns. I have ordered three ball gowns as well. The first will be for the Lynford Ball. Wait till you see it. It is beautiful beyond words."

"Mara, you will let me know how much I owe you for these." Nicola made a sweeping gesture to the bed.

Nicola received an allowance each month, which was more than she needed. Her foster mother had taught her early in life to invest her income each year and her wealth had grown. She took great pleasure in using her funds for the betterment of the less fortunate, most often abandoned women and their children.

"Nicola, the pleasure is all mine."

She started to protest.

"Wait," Mara interjected. "Let me finish. I told you

my dress shop is successful. It is flourishing. I am making more money than I know what to do with. So I am sharing the wealth, so to speak." Mara continued to unpack boxes and place garments on the bed. "You continue to do your good work with your herbs, teaching the children, and I will continue to do what I do best—letting the *Ton* pay high prices for my creations."

Nicola hung her new Spencer jacket in the wardrobe. Mara walked out into the hallway and waited for her sister.

"Wait, my new clothes." Nicola joined Mara. "I will never be able to get into bed."

"Sally will come and put them away." Mara patted her sister's arm.

Walking down the stairs together in silence, Nicola enjoyed the quiet of just being together.

"I will be in the healing room. Come. My classes are getting bigger, and I could use some help."

"Did you forget I was the worst student? I hated geography and Latin. And how did you attract more students?"

"Well, it seems word travels, like my herbal healing did. I can't say no to someone who needs my help."

"What is going to happen when you leave and go back home?"

"I do not know. We'll have to wait and see."

Mara shook her head as she watched Nicola walk to the healing room and went back into the kitchen.

Nicola was surprised at the number of people in the room. She counted them, twelve in all. The boys outnumbered the girls and some were adults.

"You invited two people?" Nicola walked over to Jeb.

"Yes, miss and them two invited more." Jeb looked down at the floor.

"It will be fine, Jeb," she whispered.

Reaching down, she took his chin in her hand and pulled it upward so she could look in his eyes. She smiled and winked at him.

"Is there enough room for everyone?"

Some of the people were sitting on the floor, while others stood against the outside wall.

This room won't be big enough after tonight. I will have to look for a larger one.

"All of you are welcome to stay and learn. All I ask is that you do not laugh at anyone else's progress. Everyone learns in their own way and time." She paused.

Heads nodded in agreement.

"We do not have enough supplies so we will have to share. Next time we meet, I will have acquired additional books and slates."

Eel entered the room after taking Janey Ann home. Nicola sent him to ask Mara for help as there were too many people to work within the small space.

She wrote everyone's name in a leather bound book and talked to each person to find out their strengths, what they hoped to learn, and why they were there. They all agreed to meet two evenings a week for two hours beginning the next week.

After all the students left, Nicola dropped exhausted into a chair. She planted her elbows on the table and rested her head on the palms of her open hands. Mara sat across from her.

"Thank you for helping. I know you did not want to."

"In truth I enjoyed it and besides, you are to be my model. Seems like a fair trade to me." Mara said, "I wonder how you managed to get so involved with people here in such a short time. I mean you just arrived and already you are so busy. You astound me, you always have."

"I cannot answer you, it just happens." Nicola shook her head. "Did you ever see so many people wanting to learn? I hope I can find a bigger place to hold classes. In fact, I wonder…"

"Pray tell, what is going through that head of yours? I can hear the wheels turning."

"Do you think it would be possible to start a real school, with a knowledgeable teacher? Teaching three lads is one thing. I can teach the basics, but I cannot do what these people need. This time, I am in over my head."

"For once I might be able to help you. One of my friends is looking for something to do besides dance, sew, and look for a husband she does not want." Mara placed her hands on the table. "She is like us, on the shelf, a very forward thinking woman, and she might be interested in this type of project."

"Excellent." Nicola's exhaustion evaporated. "Do you think we could go and see her first thing in the morning? We could send Eel with a message."

"Sister Dear, you are brilliant. In fact, my dress shop shall sponsor the school. Creations will buy a building and pay for the supplies."

"We need a name," Nicola said, as her excitement grew. "We shall have a contest among the students."

Chapter Seventeen

As the days sped by, Nicola caught glimpses of Clay Barber when she was out shopping and sightseeing. Were her eyes deceiving her? Had he been there or not? Did he spy on her? Her thoughts were always on him. Was that why she saw him everywhere? There were so many unanswered questions.

Mara's friend, Samantha Webster, took over the learning lessons with speed and determination. She took charge and promised to run over anyone in her way. A building was purchased within two days, renovations were underway, and the school was in full session. There were daytime classes for children and night classes for anyone who could not attend then. Sam hired three teachers for "The Learning Place" (TLP) as the school was called. Nicola and Mara were on the board of directors.

George vanished, as had his pilfering friends who included Mr. Pagger. Emmy's problem, for the moment, had either been postponed or taken care of with the disappearance of the thieves. Time would tell. Nicola was willing to wait and see.

Now she had the time to pursue her lost parents in earnest. Being raised in a rural area had given her little opportunity. It took months to receive replies to the letters she sent out, and many times the responses gave her more questions. But now she was in London and didn't want to waste a minute because she had no idea how much longer she would stay in the greatest city in England.

Nicola did not know what dress she would be wearing for the Winter Ball. But her jewelry would include her signet ring and the earrings her parents had left her. Someone might recognize them and be able to provide answers to her many questions about her birth family.

"You will see your beautiful gown the night of the ball." Mara stood just inside Nicola's bedroom door. "Susan is so busy making dresses, I had to hire additional staff."

"Well that is grand." Nicola frowned. "What if I do not like it or it does not get done in time. Or will not fit me?"

"Not a dress I designed. You know my designs are over the top."

"Modest you are not," Nicola stated. "Oh, I am sorry. It is…oh fustian! I would just as soon stay home. I hate the crush of people."

"How can you hate something you have never been to?"

Nicola stuck her tongue out at Mara and stomped over to the chair.

"That wasn't very lady like." Mara shook her head and tried to hide her smile behind her hand. She cleared her throat. "This is not a country dance. The men you have met, since coming to London, are the ones you doctor up from either street fighting or manual labor. They are not bad people, but they…" Mara walked further into the room and sat on the desk chair. "You need to be seen by the *Ton*. It will do you good. Besides

Aunt Belle would be so disappointed if we did not go. She has been practicing her dancing."

"You are jesting?" Nicola studied Mara's face. When she noticed her sister's lips start to turn up, she started to giggle. "You are, aren't you?"

"No, I saw her last night. She and her maid practice most afternoons and evenings. It was a sight to behold. She even went through her entire wardrobe looking for a decent dress. I offered to have one made, but she said she wanted to wear Uncle William's favorite, which, I might add is so out of date."

"It must be green," Nicola said.

"No, it's lavender and not a very good color for her. It is the last party dress Uncle William saw her in."

"Do not tell me she is going to change her favorite color to lavender again."

"That was her favorite before pink, or it might have been before yellow." Mara laughed until tears ran down her face.

****

Nicola had almost forgotten how long it took to get ready. If she heard Winter Fantasy Ball or Lynford's name once more, she swore she would scream. First, her bath. Everyone thought she should sit and soak in the water until her skin looked old and wrinkled. Well, her idea was get in the tub, wash, and get out. Sitting by the fire, she dried her hair. It was so pleasant and quiet. It reminded her of her small, cozy cottage in Chew Magna. She never had time to sit and enjoy the fire. She took such pleasure in it she fell sound asleep until Mara shook her awake.

"Pray stop. You will give me a headache."

"I thought you were in your bath, and what do I

find?"

"I am relaxing, enjoying the quiet before the parade."

"Parade? Is there to be a parade? Where, when?"

Nicola snickered. "Not an actual parade, silly goose. Everyone parades around in their finery, doing their best to outdo everyone else. Do you not remember Mrs. Zentner at the country parties back home? She always dressed to the nines. She tried so hard to look the height of fashion."

"How could I forget that evil woman? After you caught her stealing my designs, when she came to visit Catherine, we did not get invited again. Well, this ball is going to be enjoyable. You wait and see." Mara shook her head. "I will bring your dress in a few minutes."

Sally arrived to arrange her hair in a profusion of full curls placed high on the top of her head. A tiara of pearls and white crepe roses sat far back amongst the curls. Nicola moved to look at herself in the mirror.

"Why is the mirror covered, may I ask?" Nicola looked at the other mirror on the far side of the room. It too had a sheet over it.

"Your sister wants to surprise you." Sally curtsied. "Miss Mara does not want you to look at yourself until you be completely dressed, miss."

Nicola opened the wardrobe in her room. She wanted to find comfort by touching the old, familiar garments she wore during the day. They were all gone. She quickly moved to the dresser and looked in a drawer for her favorite undergarments. Everything had been replaced with all the items Mara continued to bring home. Not a day went by her sister didn't bring her something new.

I am going to strangle Mara the first chance I get.

Mara kicked open the bedroom door with her foot. "Sorry, did I startle you?"

Nicola didn't say a word, she glared.

"Sally, are you ready? Now, Nicola, please stand with your eyes closed so we can get you into this dress. I know you are going to be the belle of the ball."

"Why do I have to close my eyes?" But Nicola still shut them as commanded. "I cannot see what I look like. You covered the mirrors."

Why oh why did I agree to any of this nonsense?"

"Humor me, Sister Dear. Keep them closed, please?"

The yards of soft material floated over her head and glided down her body. Sally buttoned the small buttons down the back of the dress. Floating around Nicola, Mara touched the dress here and there.

"Sally, take the covering off the large mirror. Sister Dear, you can open your eyes."

Nicola slowly opened one eye, then the other. Her eyes widened as she looked at her reflection. A beautiful woman stared back. The hunter green dress was magnificent. Its short puffed sleeves were trimmed in white roses and pearls to match her tiara. She turned around slowly, never taking her eyes off her reflected image. She even pinched herself to make sure she wasn't in a dream.

Mara and Sally stood off to one side to watch. Emmy joined them.

"Nicola, you are as beautiful as I knew you would be. You were right about the pastels, they might be the rage this season but not on you. This color suits you,"

Mara said.

Knocking on the door interrupted them. Aunt Belle swished into the room in a light lavender dress. A matching hat with a large feather was perched on her head.

"Gels, you all look so beautiful. I have something for each of you. Catherine would be so proud if she were here, where she belongs. Why she lives in the middle of nowhere is beyond me." Aunt Belle clapped her hands together and then tapped her fan on the table to get everyone's undivided attention. "Our dear Mara has quite a flair for dress designing."

"I agree." Nicola twirled in place. "I feel like a princess."

Aunt Belle's face flushed with excitement as she handed each niece a leather case. A necklace and earrings, which matched each of their ball gowns, lay nestled in soft black velvet. Nicola received emeralds, Mara rubies, and Emmy diamonds.

"Dear ones"—Aunt Belle silenced them with a wave of her hand—"these were gifts from my dear departed husband." She grasped her hands together. "I received them with love, and I give them with love. My fondest wish is you will remember your dear Aunt Belle each time you wear them. Please pass them on to your daughters." Tears welled in her eyes as the women rushed to give her a hug.

"Now gels, you must not wrinkle your beautiful dresses." Aunt Belle wiped her eyes with the handkerchief Mara handed to her. "It is time we are off."

Mara and Emmy, with the help of Sally put their necklaces and earrings in place.

"Dear Aunt Belle, would you be offended if I wore just the necklace?" Nicola took her aunt's hand. "You see I have on my mother's earrings."

"My dear gel, say no more. Your earrings will look wonderful with the necklace."

Everyone took a turn at the uncovered mirror.

"Aunt Belle, how did you know the necklaces you chose would match our dresses?" Emmy asked.

"I still have my ways to gather information even if I am old. Come, our carriage awaits."

Nicola welcomed the silent ride in the carriage. She and her sisters had only attended small, country parties. Due to the circumstances of their births, none of them had a coming out season in London. In truth, none of them had wanted or admitted to wanting one. Nicola considered Mara's excitement at receiving the invitation to the Winter Ball and wondered why she had never expressed a desire for a London season. She would ask her, maybe tomorrow. The closer they got to the Lynford estate the level of enthusiasm for the evening grew as did the chit-chat of the women.

The house was all aglow against the dark sky as they joined the waiting line to exit from their carriage. Men dressed in the livery of the Lynford family escorted them to the main entrance of the mansion. People's voices, the sound of music, and gentle laughter greeted them at the door.

Lord Malcolm Lynford, first in the receiving line, was followed by his current hostess. His unmarried status gave him the opportunity to choose different women for each function he orchestrated in London. It was considered, by some, an honor to be chosen by him.

Polite with all his guests, he observed protocol until his introduction to Nicola. He took her hand and brought it to his lips. Shocked he would be so bold, Nicola was surprised when he asked her to save him a dance.

"Who is she? Did you see him? What a surprise. Do you think a romance is in the offering?" The gossip followed the Highbridge women as they left the reception line.

"I wonder what that was all about, my dear," Aunt Belle whispered, walking up to Nicola.

"I do not know. I never met the man until tonight."

"Well, dear gel, you are causing quite a stir."

Reactions to Lord Lynford's actions continued to whirl around her. Nicola nudged Mara and Emmy to walk ahead of her and Aunt Belle. She used her opened fan to hide her face as she scrutinized people's reactions.

The moment they got into the ballroom, the flow of people lessened and Nicola felt more at ease. They found a chair for Aunt Belle in the chaperone gallery and guided her to it.

"I had forgotten the closeness of these affairs." Aunt Belle used her fan. "At least in here we can breathe some fresh air."

It didn't take long for the dandies to notice the three unattached women. An old friend of Aunt Belle's husband introduced his nephew and cousin. A business associate of her late husband arrived with his grandson and granddaughter. A few acquaintances were slow to come to visit, then people came in larger numbers. Everyone wanted to meet the young and very pretty Highbridge women. Over the years, most had heard about them, but had never met them.

Nicola couldn't remember who went with whom and trying to recall their titles was near impossible. She spent her first hour meeting people and feared her face would be frozen in a smile forever.

"My dear ladies." Lord Bradley bowed. "Would any of you be interested in a cool drink?"

They all agreed as the room was stuffy and warm with all the bodies pressed into the ballroom. He returned with two young friends carrying their cups of punch. The dancing began and Nicola found herself in constant demand. She whirled around the room so many times she lost count. Every time a dance ended she found herself scooped up by a different partner.

Aunt Belle sat, enjoyed the festivities, and kept a sharp eye on her girls. The rules of the *Ton* were strict and intolerant.

"Who is she? Where is she from?" The whispers followed Nicola.

After a dreadful dance when her partner stepped on her toes every other step, Nicola found a vacant chair next to Aunt Belle. She sat down to catch her breath and watch until she sensed someone staring right through her. She scanned the crowd on the far side of the dance floor until she found her host, Malcolm Lynford. Uneasy, she lowered her eyes.

Was he looking at her or someone else?

"Aunt Belle, I have to find the necessary. May I get you anything?"

"No, dear, do not tarry too long."

Spying a small, secluded alcove with an unoccupied bench, she sat down. A man reeking of whiskey fell into her lap. She jumped up. The man fell to the floor.

"I say, miss, do you think you could help me? It seems you pushed me to the floor."

"You fell." She reached to help him up, but he tried to pull her down next to him. She kicked his leg hard. He yelped and let go of her hand.

"I say. Now you have kicked me."

"You, sir, are in your cups."

Not wanting to create a scene, she hurried away but glanced back to make sure he wasn't hurt from his fall. A man was reaching down to give a helping hand. She rubbed her eyes. It looked like Mr. Barber.

Mr. Barber is a common laborer. He would not have received an invitation to such an elegant affair. There goes my mind again. Seeing what I want to see.

Her mind on Clay Barber, she ran right into Lord Lynford. He steadied her by taking her arm.

"My dear, I have been looking for you. I believe our dance is about to start." The warmth of his smile never reached his eyes. Shuddering at his touch, she moved backward and twisted to the side forcing him to release her.

Chapter Eighteen

"Sir, I must attend to my aunt," Nicola stated.

"We will see to her together, my dear." He grasped her elbow. "I must get her permission for us to do a waltz. You do know how to do the newest dance?"

"I do. It has been a rather long time since I have done so."

"I insist you call me Malcolm. I believe formalities with ladies are so unnecessary in this modern day and age." He led her to the chaperone gallery.

Aunt Belle watched to ensure her darling nieces did not get caught up in any gossip and become the latest on-dit of the *Ton.* Everyone in the room scrutinized who danced with whom and waited for any misstep.

Aunt Belle's closed fan swung back and forth in time to the music. Her left shoe peeked out from beneath the hem of her dress and tapped the same rhythm. Lord Lynford stopped directly in front and blocked her view of the dancers.

"My dear, I would like to dance a waltz with my—" Malcolm quickly took Aunt Belle's unoccupied hand. "I would be honored if your niece would dance with me. The waltz is my favorite."

"Waltzes are frowned upon in London." Aunt Belle tapped her fan on the arm of her chair.

"Belle, do not worry your pretty head." He added,

patting her hand, "Almack's is the only place the waltz is not done. This is my party. No one will tell what I can and cannot do at my Winter Ball. I will take full responsibility for our dance and will return her safe and sound." He propelled Nicola onto the dance floor before Belle could protest further.

Lord Lynford's reputation as a rake of the first order, was such that many respectable women did not want to be associated with him. There was something about him Nicola feared; maybe it was his touch, or the way he looked at her. Her subconscious tried to caution her. When she attempted to focus on the warning, it darted away.

"Well, my dear, what do you think of my festivities?" Nicola watched the couples filling the dance floor. Malcom didn't give her a chance to respond. "I do like to see everyone dressed in their finest, trying to outmaneuver one another in vying for my attention. It makes one feel important."

"Your party appears to be an enormous success."

"I noticed your beautiful earrings. They are—unique." His hand reached toward her ear. A chill ran down Nicola's spine, and she pulled her head out of reach.

"The stones come alive when they catch the candle light. May I ask how you obtained them?"

"They were a birthday gift from my mother."

"Do you happen to know where they were purchased?"

Nicola was distracted as a couple danced past them. The man looked like Mr. Barber, but it could not be.

Lynford squeezed her hand tightly to get her

attention.

"I am sorry. I was distracted by the other dancers." She tried to smile but couldn't.

"After the dance I would like to draw a picture of them, my dear."

He whirled her around and around on the floor, which put an end to all conversation. When the dance ended, Lord Lynford steered her toward the library. His grip on her arm was tight, and she was forced to go with him or create a scene. Nicola was relieved, two couples sat before the fireplace having a private chat, while others milled around the huge room. He sat at the desk and motioned to the chair across from him.

"Turn your head a little to the left so I may see your earrings more clearly." He took a piece of paper from the side desk drawer and began to sketch.

"What is the purpose of the drawing?" Nicola asked.

"With your continued chatter, I cannot concentrate on what I am doing," he scolded her. "Be quiet and still."

She sat motionless, listened to the undistinguishable voices in the room, and found some comfort in their presence.

"Please look, my dear, and see if I have the pattern correct."

She picked up the paper and held it close to the lamp on the desk.

"I don't think it is quite right." She frowned. "May I change it?"

"Are you telling me my drawing is off the mark?" Anger seeped into his words.

"No sir, it is…" She paused, trying to find the right

words. "Well, the outline is not quite in proportion. You see, I have drawn them many times over the years."

She removed her gloves, picked up the pencil, and bent over the paper. She drew the pattern as easily as writing her name. He quickly took her hand and peered intently at her right ring finger.

"My dear, I must say. Could you, a woman, actually be wearing a signet ring?"

"Yes it is an exact copy of my father's ring. Also a birthday gift." She pulled her hand from his tight grip.

"Your parents gave you unique gifts. I would like to meet them."

"I am afraid it is not possible. You see, my parents—"

Nicola was relieved when a servant interrupted them. She found it hard not to answer his questions truthfully, which caused her even more discomfort than his earlier stares.

While Lord Lynford dealt with the servant's queries, she looked around the room. Bookshelves lined the walls from floor to ceiling. She wished she had the time to browse and touch each and every volume. A large picture at the end of the room piqued her interest. A man leaned against an old castle wall. He seemed familiar but she could not place him. She had started to move toward the portrait when Lord Lynford appeared at her elbow.

"My dear, we must return. Midnight buffet will be announced soon." He smiled, as they turned their backs on the portrait. "No one can partake of the marvelous food I have provided until I, the host, lead the way."

They walked out into the hallway, which led back to the main ballroom.

"You appear upset, or are you angry for some reason?" Lynford reached for her arm.

She ignored him. Nicola had no desire to confront her host and planned to stay out of his way for the remainder of the evening.

"Sir, who are the men coming down the stairs?"

"The man dressed in black is the Earl of Woodhaven, and the dandy in the yellow coat is Jonas Wilson." Lynford said with distain, after he glanced in their direction. "Neither has any sense of fashion." He ran his hand over his puce jacket to smooth the wrinkles over his bulk. "Wilson is a rather common man. Parents are successful shop owners."

"The Earl is—" Nicola held her breath.

"Clayton Barber, you mean? He fancies himself a soldier. His father is the Duke of St. George. He acts as common as his friend. Why do you ask?"

"No reason, I—"

"Malcolm, darling, there you are," a shrill voice rang out. "It is time for your marvelous food. We must lead our guests to the dining room." His hostess for the evening swooped in and claimed her prey.

Nicola took the opportunity to escape. She had to find Mr. Barber. He was an Earl. He had lied to her and her family. She skirted around the edge of the room, saw him going out a door, and followed him.

As she stepped out of the room, two big hands grabbed her and pulled her around the edge of the house where no one could see. One hand covered her mouth so she couldn't scream.

She bit down hard on the first flesh she found, which proved to be the side of his palm near his thumb. Her captor gave a low growl.

"I am not going to harm you. We need to talk." Mr. Barber rubbed his hand. "You did not have to bite me!"

"You did not have to manhandle me," she retorted. "You are the lowest man I have ever met, and you are not what you appear to be." She perched her hands on her hips. "Are you? A common laborer I think not. Not with the title of the Earl of Woodhaven. You are the biggest—"

"Still have not found a name for me I see." He stood to the side so she couldn't leave. "I am not a common laborer. I never told you I was." He stopped talking long enough to put her hand in his. "You judged me by my clothes. You never asked me what I did, and I told you. You have no idea who or what I am. Nor do I think you care. I have been busy these last days on something you would not understand."

"You lied by omission. You never introduced yourself using your title." She hurried back into the ballroom trying to remain calm.

Chapter Nineteen

Aunt Belle, Mara, and Emmy gathered their chairs into a circle to discuss the evening. The two sisters' feet were sore from dancing, and they were glad to sit down and rest, as they gathered strength for the next round which would last until the wee hours of the morning.

"My dears, what is the matter with Nicola?" Aunt Belle asked.

The three women watched her approach across the room.

"She must be really upset and angry. Look at the way she is walking like a general, and her eyes are flashing. Danger, danger," Emmy warned.

"Who is the man behind her? It looks like—" Mara never completed her sentence.

Nicola came to an abrupt stop in front of them. "I have to leave now. I cannot stay."

Her sisters and Aunt Belle were not looking at her but past her. Nicola turned to see Mr. Barber moving in her direction. Thank heavens, someone stopped him every few steps. At the rate he traveled, he would never reach her before she left. Nicola didn't want him to cause a commotion.

"It appears something is amiss. Might I be of assistance?" Lord Lynford appeared next to the women.

Without thinking Nicola said, "I have a most dreadful headache and wish to return home." She pressed her lips together and kept her fisted hands hidden in the folds of her dress.

"I will have my carriage brought around immediately." He snapped his fingers and a servant arrived. "I would hate for the rest of you to miss the food. The menu is exotic, if I do say so myself." He stood smug and confident next to Nicola.

"Dear Malcolm, these old bones have had enough. It has been enjoyable. However, I had forgotten now tiring all this is. We shall all go home together," said Aunt Belle.

In no time at all, they were in their own hired carriage and on their way. Nicola only half listened to the chatter about the ball. As the carriage pulled into the street, Nicola thought she caught a glimpse of Mr. Barber.

"Did you notice the violet dress on the woman with dark hair? She is my best customer. To be truthful, many women were wearing Creations fashions." Mara rubbed her gloved hands together.

"Did you see the lady flirting with the Russian prince?" Aunt Belle tapped her fan on the side of the carriage. "Disgraceful. That young lady will be the talk of the *Ton* tomorrow. Mark my words."

"What about our Nicola doing the waltz? I thought it was not to be done," Emmy said.

"Since so many of the other guests chose to do the waltz, I did not see any harm in her following the others. After all, her partner was the host." Aunt Belle started to hum a tune from the party.

"I was amused," Emmy said. "The music and the dancing were divine, and observing the people provided offered a great deal of amusement."

"Did you know—?"

Nicola blocked out Aunt Belle's voice. All she wanted to do was envision Mr. Barber. She settled back against the soft leather, closed her eyes, and pictured him—so handsome, dressed in black with a white shirt and cravat. Her mind cleared the minute the carriage stopped. She once again heard the chatter of her sisters and Aunt Belle. The outrider helped them down and walked them to the door.

"I would like a cup of tea. Anyone else care to join me?" Mara asked, after they entered the house. "I am hungry after all the dancing."

"These old bones are off to bed," declared Aunt Belle.

The three sisters agreed tea and whatever food the cook left out for them were in order. Cook surprised them with cakes and small ham breads. Nicola only had to add hot water to the teapot, which sat on the center of the table, to complete their repast.

"All right Nicola, tell me, tell us, was your Mr. Barber following you at the ball?" Mara asked.

Nicola ignored her sister's question.

"You know, the handsome man dressed in black." Mara pushed the sugar bowl toward her sister.

"He is not my Mr. Barber, in fact he is—" A knock on the door interrupted her. She sighed and quickly opened it.

Two men stood before her and by the looks of them, they were from Bow Street. Their clothes were dirty and torn. Bruises, small cuts, and scrapes covered their faces. She recognized the taller of the men. Earlier in the week, she had treated Jenson for a knife wound.

"Sorry to bother you, miss. Pete had a bit of bad

luck and needs you to look at his side. We only come because we seen the light."

"I must change first." She ushered the men into the hallway and into the healing room. "Pete, please lie down on the table. I will return in a few minutes."

"I'll bring you all some tea." Mara stood.

"That would be wonderful." Nicola hurried out of the room.

She scampered to the servant stairway, which was just off the kitchen, and looked about. When she saw no one, she grabbed a handful of her dress below the waist, pulled it up, and ran up the stairs. Sally undressed her faster than she thought possible.

Upon her return downstairs, she stopped in the kitchen, took a pot of hot water kept on the stove for emergencies, and hurried back to the injured man. But first, she took a clean apron from the wooden pegs on the back of the door and put it on.

"Jenson, help Pete off with his coat and shirt. I have to gather my supplies." Nicola went to the cupboard, gathered her herbs and her stitching kit."

"I could not get his shirt off. Part of it is in the wound." Jenson grimaced.

"I am going to have to cut your shirt."

"It-it be the only one I got, miss."

"There is no way this shirt can be mended." Nicola pointed to the four-inch-long, blood and dirt-matted tear, which ran down the right side from sleeve to hem.

"Do what you must." Pete hung his head.

"There are still some of uncle's shirts about." Mara had walked in during the conversation. She set down three cups of steaming tea on the table. "I will see if I can find them."

Nicola took over. "Pete, I want you on the covered table. It will be easier for me to stitch your side." Once he was settled, she cleaned the wound and stitched it. By the time Mara returned with the shirts, she had wrapped the wound and cleaned both men's faces.

"I am not sure the shirts will fit so I brought a couple. I found two jackets too. I thought you could both use them. Your own clothes seem to have gotten...well, quite ruined in the process of your night's work."

"We do not take handouts," Jenson said.

"Who said anything about a handout?" Mara straightened her shoulders and looked at both men. "I expect both of you to work for the clothes. You can start when next you have time off from your work. Believe me, plenty of odd jobs here need to be done."

The door opened. "Well, what have we here?" Clay asked. "Every time I see you, Jenson, you have been in a fight. Do you not do any other duties at Bow Street?"

"Fights do seem to find me, sir. Comes with the job. Stopped a robbery this 'ere fine night. Three against two. Turned into a brawl, it did."

"The foot pads be in worse shape than us and by now be sitting in Newgate, nursing their wounds," Pete added.

Nicola gave the man instructions for care of his wound, bandages, and herbal tinctures, and told him to come back in a week.

"I need to speak with you." Clay sat down at the table next to Nicola who had a teacup in her hand. "I have to explain."

"I do not think I care."

"Gentlemen, if you will excuse us." Clay gently

unhooked her fingers from the cup.

As the men reached the outside door, it slammed against the inside wall. A man staggered into the room. His hand held onto the edge of the door.

"Miss, we needs 'elp."

The man moved away from the door still trying to catch his breath. He bent over at the waist and gasped "My wife be 'aving 'ard time birthing our babe."

Nicola guided the man further into the room and with care pushed him into a chair. "Sit down while I get my belongings." She took off her apron and flung it on the chair. Then she rushed out of the room to get her warmest cape and found Sally was already bringing it. The man was pacing the room.

"Please, miss, we must hurry, my wife is—"

The door opened and cold wind followed Eel into the room. "We be 'aving a celebration?"

"No, this man's wife is birthing a baby and needs my assistance."

"I'll come." Clay moved away from the warmth of the stove.

"I think not—"

"Sir," Jenson spoke up. "We be needing you to come with us."

"Eel, go with Miss Nicola and stay until she returns home." Clay said decisively.

"Yes, sir."

"Can we walk or must we find a carriage?" Nicola asked.

"It be only six streets from 'ere, faster to walk."

The mist swirled around them. The cold night enveloped them. Visibility was limited to inches, and the streets appeared ominous.

Eel wasn't sure when he first realized a carriage traveled slowly behind them. The wheels turned on the cobbles, crunching against the stones and echoed off each other. Was it being careful because in places the mist became a heavy fog or was it actually following them?

The trio walked fast. The man broke into a run numerous times and then slowed down only to run again after a few paces.

When they reached the house, the sound of the wheels stopped. In fact, the carriage never passed them. It stayed well behind.

Eel walked into the house behind the others. A few red embers glowed from an old stove in the corner of the room. Three small children huddled on a faded, broken down, oversized chair sitting mere inches from the heat. A woman moaned in another room. Nicola and the man moved toward the sound.

Eel found a small amount of coal, lifted off the plate on the top of the stove, and added it to the fire. Getting down on his hands and knees, he blew into the grate until small flames licked at the new fuel source. The children watched Eel's every move. He tried to talk to them, but they just stared. The man re-appeared.

"Miss would like to see you." He gestured for Eel to follow him.

When Eel entered the room, Nicola was leaning over the woman in bed and whispering to her.

"Eel, make sure there is plenty of hot water on the stove and mind the children. It will not be long now."

He nodded his head and walked back to the children. "Don't you be worried. Miss Nicola be taking good care of your mother and the new babe when it be borned."

After filling a banged up pot with water, he placed it on the stove. While he waited, he stood at the window and stared into the night. The outline of the carriage was still there. It had not moved closer. The fog was gone, but mist still swirled in the air. He walked back to the stove, added a few more scrapes of coal, and then perched himself on the arm of the chair. It was a short time before he noticed the children, all three of them, had moved over and were now sitting as close to him as they could get. His mind, however, kept going back to the carriage.

The two little girls fell asleep. He covered them with a threadbare blanket he picked up off the floor.

"I got to go talk to someone." He looked at the boy. "Tell the lady to wait until I gets back before 'er leaves. She *must* wait for me."

The boy nodded his head.

The carriage still hadn't moved. Eel left by the back door and ran through the mews behind the houses. He didn't want to be seen. He hoped Mr. Barber had returned to Miss Nicola's house, but the house was completely dark and locked up tight.

Nicola settled everyone. When the new baby boy and his proud parents were asleep, she walked to the front of the house and found all three children, huddled together in the big chair.

The boy woke up, looked at her. "Boy be back, wait," he mumbled.

Talking about Eel, she supposed. He'd got tired and left.

She tried to question the young boy, but he had fallen back into a sound sleep. Nicola tucked the children in with a second blanket she found in their parents' bedroom in the hopes it would ward off the cold seeping into the house. She scraped in and around the almost empty coal bin and built up the fire hoping it would last until morning. She would have coal delivered tomorrow. A gift from an anonymous friend.

She left the house and started the walk home. She thought of Mr. Barber, which wasn't unusual. It seemed he was all she thought about, at least most of the time. She smiled to herself. Clay looked so handsome at the ball. Yet they couldn't be in a room for five minutes without arguing about something. And he was always trying to order her about.

She stopped at the corner to put on her gloves before she crossed the street. A carriage pulled up in front of her blocking her way. Before she could react, the door was flung open and large hands yanked her inside. It happened so fast. Before the coach started to move again, Nicola was unconscious.

****

Eel banged on the door of the small run down house.

"Quit the racket. I am coming," a voice called out.

When the door flew open, Eel stared with disappointment. Barnaby stood with a candle in one hand and a gun in the other. "I needs to find Mr. Barber."

"I am not his keeper, boy." Barnaby motioned Eel into the house. "Rather early to be here, ain't it."

Halfway through Eel's concerns about the carriage, Barnaby and the boy left the house to begin their search for Clay. They tried the Owl Tavern and two gaming halls. They found him at last, back at his house on

North Hampton.

"Where 'ave you been? We be"—Eel marched up to Clay—"been looking everywhere for you. Miss Nicola, 'er be in trouble."

"What the hell are you talking about?" Clay grabbed him by the front of his coat until their faces were mere inches apart. "She is delivering a baby."

Eel quickly repeated the story about the carriage. Clay let go of Eel's coat, turned, and left the house slamming the door behind him. It didn't take long for Eel to be out of breath trying to keep up with Mr. Barber's long strides. He only managed by half walking and half running. Barnaby was a good two blocks behind them when they got to the Smiths' house.

Eel grabbed Mr. Barber's arm. "Wait. You cannot be pounding on the door. There be a new baby. I'll go and see if her still be 'ere. You stay outside or you be scaring the children."

Eel went to the side yard and found the door unlocked like he left it. He crept inside listening for voices, noises, any sound which could mean Nicola was still in the house. He even peeked in the small bedroom where the parents and the new baby were asleep. The children were still huddled near the stove. He left the house the way he entered and found Clay standing in front of the window.

"She not be 'ere, sir. Everyone be asleep. It be my fault. I should 'ave stayed with 'er." Eel blinked away his tears.

"Perhaps she went home another way." Clay pointed to the street to the west. "You go down that street. I will take the street to the east and meet you back at the Highbridge house."

Chapter Twenty

Clay hoped Nicola would be waiting for him. He planned to wring her neck after he kissed her. He silently offered a prayer to the heavens above for her safekeeping. It was the first time since his brother's untimely death he had uttered a heavenly thought for anything or anyone.

I love her. I really love her.

The thought struck him hard as a punch in the stomach. Panic struck at him. He couldn't think, and his stomach felt like it had been replaced with a solid rock.

Eel stood waiting for him at the Highbridge back gate.

"No sign of her, sir."

"Well, she could be safely in the house." Clay repeatedly knocked on the front door until Sally peeked out.

She opened the door and motioned them in. "Who do you want to see?" She rubbed her eyes and pulled her shawl around her shoulders.

"What is happening?" Mara demanded, as she stood on the top landing. "And who is hammering on the door and making enough noise to wake even me?" She gathered her robe round herself, descended the stairs, and stopped right in front of Clay. She looked at him with raised eyebrows. "I am sure you can explain all this?"

"Is Nicola here?" He gave her a slight bow. "She left the Smith house after delivering the baby."

"Oh, now I remember," Mara said with a sigh.

"Please, Miss Mara." Eel stuck his hands in his jacket pockets. "Could we be going where it be warm?"

"Oh my, yes. Let us go into the kitchen. I can guarantee Cook has a fire going to raise her morning bread. Would you both like some tea, while we wait for Nicola?" Mara signaled them to follow her.

Looking at Eel, Clay put his finger to his lips. They both sat while Mara made tea.

"I am sure Nicola will be here at any moment." Mara gathered day old breads and sweets for them to eat. "Someone probably stopped her on the way home. You would be amazed at the amount of people who come here." Mara studied their faces. "Why do I get the feeling there is more to this? The two of you look like you lost your best friend."

Clay was having a difficult time sitting there when he wanted to be out scouring the streets looking for his Nicola. But he had learned in his government career it was best to form a plan of action and gather all the facts. Organization took less time than running around in circles, and in the long run accomplished much more in a shorter period. So he sat and tried to think and plan while Mara talked.

"Well, Miss Mara, we have lost Miss Nicola." Eel shuffled his feet. "Her were followed again." Eel didn't look at Mara. His guilt kept him staring at the floor.

"What do you mean followed? This has happened more than once? You are scaring me half to death."

Without stopping for a breath, Clay related the story about the carriage and Eel's fear.

"I told the boy to tell Miss Nicola not to leave until I come back." Eel still could not look at the adults in the room.

"Unfortunately, it took him a while to find me. When we got to the Smith house, she was gone. So was the carriage." Clay stood. "We each followed a different route here, but there is no sign of her or anyone else."

A sudden knock caused Mara to drop her teacup. It broke and the contents spilled in all directions. Eel looked up from the floor. Clay jumped up and held the door open as Barnaby wandered into the kitchen.

"About time you got here." Clay could not keep the disappointment from his voice. He had hoped Nicola would be standing in the entrance wondering why everyone was so upset.

"When you hurry you fail to notice important clues." Barnaby held up a glove. "I found this a half a block from the Smith house. It was on the corner. Does it look familiar to you?" He handed it to Mara.

She took it from Barnaby's outstretched hand. "This is one of Nicola's gloves. Where is the other one?"

"How can you be so sure?" Clay closed the door.

"I made a pair of them, my one and only attempt. They were so poorly constructed." Mara shook her head. "But Nicola said they would be fine and took them. I promised never to make another glove, and I have not. She actually told me they were very valuable. They were one of a kind." Mara started to cry.

"Clay will find her." Barnaby handed her a handkerchief and patted her hand. "Do not worry, Miss Mara."

"Barnaby, get the Runners, Eel, you fetch Jeb and Jimmy. It is time to begin a search. Someone had to hear or see something."

Mara dried her tears. "We will clean the mess from the floor, make food to eat, and, of course, more tea," Mara squeezed her hands together. "I will get Cook."

"Before you leave could I please have a pen and paper?" Clay asked. "I need to make a few maps so everyone knows where the search area is."

Clay had completed the maps by the time Barnaby returned with four Bow Street Runners, all of whom had received medical care from Nicola. Eel with his mates and his mother, Susan, followed hard on their heels.

Susan and Mara were to stay at the house and help in any way they could. Clay gave each man a map of the area they were to search. They all agreed to meet back in two hours, and then Clay all but pushed each man out the door. He promised food and tea when they returned.

"Good luck and Godspeed." Mara stood in the doorway, dabbing her eyes with a towel as she tried to hold back the tears.

Jeb stayed behind in case Nicola came home. It would be his job to round up all the searchers. All arrived back at the house on time except Eel. Everyone was cold, tired, and hungry.

The street by now was alive with people so they questioned everyone they met. No one had seen or heard anything. Everyone sat around the table, while Clay paced back and forth and discussed their next plan of action. He knew they had to stay organized to find Nicola.

"I wonder if her disappearance could have anything to do with her search for her birth parents?" Mara asked without thinking.

"Why would she be hunting for her parents?" Clay asked.

"Because she never knew them." Mara sighed. "Our parents, for whatever reasons, gave Nicola, Emmy, and myself to Catherine Highbridge to raise. It has become very important for Nicola to know who her birth parents are. And since she is here in London and Emmy's problem appears to be resolved, she decided it would be the ideal time to see what she could find out."

"Why is it so important?"

"Her reasons are her own," Mara said. "You will have to ask her."

"But how did she expect to find them?" Clay rubbed his thumb along his chin line as he listened.

"She has a signet ring and extraordinary earrings. They were gifts left for her eighteenth birthday." Mara bit her lower lip. "They are the only clues she has."

"Do you know where she keeps them?" He set his cup down. "I would like to see them."

"Mr. Barber, I am not sure my sister would—"

"I do not plan to steal them. I want to look at them."

Mara took Sally aside and told her where the jewelry could be found. No one spoke while they waited for the servant to return. Once Mara received the articles, she handed them to Clay who examined them.

"Do you recognize them?" Mara folded her arms.

"No. The emblem on the ring is an animal, a griffin I believe. It is hard to see as this ring is small. Yet, the ring does look familiar. I am not sure where I have seen it. I wonder…"

Eel entered with a haggard old woman following close behind.

Clay slipped the jewelry into his shirt pocket. He felt more comfort having the items close to his heart. He would return them to Mara later.

"Do not be afraid. No one here will 'arm you." Eel took the woman's arm and propelled her farther into the room. The woman moved toward the table but kept her eyes on the door. "You be telling them what you told me."

They all held their breath waiting for her to speak.

She eyed the finger cakes sitting on the table. "Are you sure I should be in this 'ere fine 'ouse?" She spoke almost in a whisper.

"Please sit here and tell your story." Clay sprang forward, cupped her elbow, and shifted her to a vacant chair. "I will get you a cup of tea and some cakes."

She smiled a toothless grin and settled back in the chair.

Mara cleared her throat but caught the shake of Clay's head and didn't open her mouth.

"You go a'ead now." Eel nodded for the old woman to continue.

"I seen the carriage that took the lady away. I were in the doorway of Mr. Fletcher's 'ouse, taking shelter. The 'ealing lady walked toward me. 'Er started to cross the street, and the carriage pulled in front of her. After the carriage left, poof, 'er was gone." The old woman drank her tea and ate her cakes.

"Who and why?" demanded Clay.

Everyone looked at Clay, waiting for him to answer his own questions. When the silence became unbearable, they all started talking at once.

Mara started to cry.

"Who would take Nicola and why?" Clay repeated. "It does not make sense."

"I know not who be in the carriage, but I know who be owning it," the old woman said, sitting up straight in the chair as she wiped her hand across her mouth.

All conversation stopped, and everyone stared at her.

"How can you know who owns the carriage?" asked one of the Runners who had come into the kitchen.

"I didn't always live on the street." Tears gathered in her eyes. "I 'ad me a daughter once, a beautiful daughter. 'Er and me darling husband, Paulie, were killed when a carriage runned them down. I lost my family, my 'ouse, our business, and were forced to live on the streets."

Clay held up his arms to stop all conversations. He knelt next to her and took the old woman's hand in his, "Please tell us who owns the carriage," he said, trying to keep his voice soft so as not to scare her. "We must find the herbal lady before anything happens to her."

The woman spat. "The carriage belongs to Malcolm Lynford." She wiped away tears that ran down her face with the back of her soiled hand leaving streaks where the dirt washed away.

"Why would he want to kidnap Nicola?" Mara shook her head. "He was very taken by her at his ball last night. It does not make any sense."

Clay's heart pounded, his throat so dry he couldn't speak. All this time he hoped she had stopped on the street and offered aid to someone who needed her herbal skills. Now it was apparent someone meant to do her harm. The time for planning was done. Action was needed—quick action.

"Wait a minute," Barnaby said. "Just because he might own the carriage does not mean he is responsible. Anyone could have been driving it."

"I agree," Mara shouted.

Everyone started talking at once. Clay slammed his fist on the table; cups and plates wobbled and clattered, but he got everyone's attention.

"All right, we have the how. The who, the why, will have to wait. The where is the most important."

Mara frowned as she asked, "The where?"

"Yes, where was she taken?"

Chapter Twenty-One

Nicola wanted to reach out and offer comfort to whoever was moaning, but she could not move. She managed to open both eyes at the same time and found she was lying on a dirt-strewn carriage floor. Her dry lips issued a protest every time she tried to shift her position or the carriage hit a bump in the road. When she could think clearly, she discovered she was the person whimpering.

Every movement caused the ache in her head to pound harder. Her hands tied behind her back and her feet bound together made it impossible to change her position, but she continued to try.

With one hand, she grabbed the foul smelling horse blanket which had been thrown over her, and pulled it downward, away from her face The movement strained her arm muscles, already cramped from being in such an awkward position. The smell of stale food combined with manure made her gag.

The carriage stopped. Nicola recognized the sound of large barn doors opening and hitting a wall like the one at the Highbridge estate. She remembered the thud when a sudden wind storm had torn them off their hinges. For a minute she thought she was back home and safe in the barn feeding the horses. The vehicle began crawling forward once again but came to a complete stop within a few feet.

"The gent said we was to keep 'er 'ere," an unfamiliar voice said.

"I be thinking we can 'ave a bit of fun with 'er. Iffin' you know what I means," another voice sneered.

"The gent said 'er was to come to no harm."

"Getting a poke at 'er will not cause any 'arm. 'Er might enjoy it."

"You want your bunt or not?"

Nicola's head hurt, but she knew it wasn't a serious injury. She must make it appear she was oblivious to what was happening around her and make her escape.

Callous hands groped at her arms. They pulled her from the carriage and stood her on the ground. The men half carried, half dragged her to the corner of an old building. They pushed her down onto a molding hay mound. The smell filled her nostrils and she sneezed. Nausea broiled in her stomach.

"You stay where we puts you, or you be real sorry, lassie," a burly man said.

She struggled to keep her mouth shut and suppress her anger. It took all her energy to give the impression she couldn't think clearly. Nicola stared at the men, and then let her eyes roll as her head fell back onto the prickly hay. Her head and arms ached. Every part of her body throbbed.

"Might be, you 'it her too 'ard," the second man whined.

She tilted her head so her eyes opened enough to see. She didn't want to miss anything. Knowledge of her surroundings gave her hope.

They were in a barn; Nicola saw the stalls in the far corner. There were three men. The driver still sat on the driving box. The two others, dockworkers by the look and smell of them, were the dirtiest men she had seen since arriving in London.

Both were average height. The burly man had gray, stringy hair. The other man appeared to be in charge. He had dark, greasy hair, tied back with a strip of leather. His face looked like an old dried prune. They grumbled, until they found part of a tabletop and two wooden crates standing against a wall. Then they cleared a space, lit a lantern, and started playing cards.

Noises filtered into the barn from outside; wagon wheels crunched on the gravel, tradespeople called one another as they filled their carts, horses were hitched to carriages. She tried to stay awake, but exhaustion and the fact she had not slept did her in.

She didn't know if she awoke from the cold or the fact the gray-headed man stood over her. Without thinking, she screamed. He grabbed her, lifted her up with one hand, and backhanded her across her mouth.

"You shut your face or I be sticking somethin' into it." He smiled, showing his rotten teeth.

He held his fist in her face and shoved it under her chin. The pressure he applied suggested he would hit her simply because he could. He let go and watched her fall. When his mate reminded him to leave her be or there would be no bunt, the man turned his back on her, and sauntered away laughing.

Nicola recoiled into the hay and shut her eyes. The side of her face stung and she could taste blood but she refused to let anyone see her cry.

****

Clay gathered Eel, Jimmy, Jeb, and the Bow Street Runners around him. "We shall meet on the corner of Howard and India Street. The area houses many carriages, carts, and the like. To me it is the logical place to start our search.

"Eel, round up as many of your street friends as you can. The more people we have, the better." The lads scampered off.

His instincts told him the carriage would still be in the city at least until nightfall. It wasn't something he could explain. He knew it was still in London. He could sense it.

There had been rumors for years about Malcolm Lynford—a power-hungry man who would stop at nothing to get what he wanted. The problem was he could not figure out how Nicola fitted into any of Lynford's plans.

Clay hurried to their meeting place, angry at himself for making earlier assumptions that Nicola was safe and detained by someone who needed her help. At this point, looking back wouldn't find her. It was a waste of time that should have been used to move forward and find his Nicola.

A man swaggered down the street and stopped in front of Clay and the Runners. "I be in charge, been sent over by the Magistrate."

"Who are you?" Clay smelled the alcohol on his breath.

Behind him the Runners whispered and moved away from the intruder.

"Mr. Booker." The man rocked back and forth on his feet, heel to toe. His chest puffed out. "I be in charge and everyone here be following me instructions to the letter."

"Listen, Booker, I am—"

"I do not care who you be. And the name is Mr.

Booker to the likes of you." He turned his back on Clay and motioned for one of the Runners to come to him. "The rest of you can get back to the Magistrates' office. I be in charge here, and we will probably find the lass with a friend, if you knows what I mean."

Clay doubled up his fist, marched over to confront the pompous Booker for the insult to his Nicola. It took two Runners to grab his jacket and hold him in place.

Eel and his friends stood a half of block away. They weren't going to come any closer, not with Booker strutting back and forth. Eel shuffled up to Clay with caution.

After a discussion with the remaining Runners, Clay, Barnaby, and Eel approached the arrogant fool.

"My young friend here might know where the carriage holding Miss Highbridge can be found." Clay clenched his teeth and thrust his fists into his pockets. What he wanted to do was punch Booker into next week.

"And when would you have seen this 'ere coach?" Booker glared at Eel.

"Last week. Me mate Sammy—"

"Too long ago. We got work to do." Booker pushed Eel aside. "You boy, take your friends"—he motioned at the youths down the street—"and you best be leaving before I have you taken to Newgate for interference. Maybe they will transport the lot of you. Good riddance if you asks me!"

Clay took Eel by the arm and pulled him down the street. They left Booker and the Runner trying to figure out what to do next.

"Come, Eel. We have work to do," Clay said. "Let us hope your friend knows what he is talking about, and the carriage he saw is the one we are looking for."

Clay, Barnaby, and Eel followed Sammy in single file to the warehouses, while Booker pondered over a map of the city. The building was empty, but a carriage had been there not long ago. Fresh wheel tracks marked the littered floor. Barnaby and Clay moved to the next block to search, and the street youth split into three groups exploring other buildings in the immediate area.

Clay looked into every barn, shed, and horse stall he walked past. Barnaby took one side of the road and he the other.

They had been searching for an hour when a whistle sounded: three short, and one long blast.

"What the hell is that?" Clay shouted to Barnaby.

"A signal, I think." Barnaby walked over to stand next to his friend.

It was the emergency signal the Rantipoles, the street gang, used. The boys all gathered around the youth who had whistled. Then as a group they moved toward the corner. Jeb motioned for them to follow. Barnaby and Clay ran to catch up, and Clay ordered them to stop.

"What is going on?" He looked at Jeb.

"We done found it. In the old barn behind the run-down theater. Eel got a plan."

"Everyone be quiet and follow Jeb," Clay commanded.

Eel and Jimmy waited two blocks away. From their vantage point, they could see the barn door.

"Jeb says you have a plan, Eel."

"I do." Eel pointed to half the group. "You make a lot of noise and fight near them front doors. When the men 'olding Miss Nicola come to watch, Mr. Barber and me be sneaking inside." He gestured toward the back of the building. "We be goin' through some rotten boards in the back."

"How many men?" Clay asked.

"Not sure, we can't be seein' in."

Clay stood for a very short time as he thought through Eel's plan. It would be the easiest way to get the men's attention, the quickest, and the safest for Nicola.

"Jeb, go get the Runners so they can arrest the men." He touched Jeb's arm. "Stay away from Booker. He is nothing but trouble. We shall get Nicola away and send the culprits to Newgate."

Clay and Barnaby looked on, amazed at Eel's ability to command the Rantipoles' respect. No one argued with the boy or tried to second-guess him.

Like the cogs of a well-oiled machine, everyone fell into place. Within minutes the area in front of the barn stood awash with lads hooting and hollering. The fight started with shoving, pushing, and then progressed to a knock down, fist swinging brawl. It took less than five minutes before the barn door opened and two men swaggered out. They stood, watched, and laughed. The lads moved and before the men knew it they were inside a circle.

Eel shifted two of the loose boards and slipped into the barn. Clay followed after he tore out two more rotten pieces of wood. The Rantipoles' racket covered any noise Clay and Eel made. Clay whispered to Eel he would take care of the man standing next to the horses. He scooped up some loose rope in the corner of the building and sneaked up on the man, knocked him out, and tied him up.

Eel moved to Nicola and cut the ropes off her hands and feet. She tried to stand but couldn't. Clay lifted her into his arms and took her out the way he had come in, but only after he kissed her. He set her on a wooden crate.

Clay smiled broadly at his Miss Nicola as he watched her rub her wrists. He stepped back to take in her appearance. He shook his head once he got a good look at her out in daylight. His prim and proper lady was gone. Part of her long hair had come loose from its confines. Hay was sticking out all over her head and covered her clothes as well. Her tear stained cheeks had washed away some of the dirt and dust that clung to her face. "Are you hurt?"

Nicola shook her head.

If he hugged her, he knew he wouldn't let her go even though she smelled like a horse stable.

He closed his eyes and took a deep breath before he kissed her again. "Eel, watch over her. I will be back." He pointed his finger at her. "You, stay here. I will be right back."

Clay hurried back through the broken boards into the barn, squeezed out the front door, and moved behind some bystanders who had gathered to watch the commotion.

"Get 'em," he hollered behind cupped hands.

The men who had held Nicola found themselves pounded into the ground. Clay let the street gang have their fun until the Runners broke it up. The boys scattered and disappeared within seconds of Booker arriving.

"I be in charge. Who done this? I should have been informed."

Clay walked up behind Booker, tapped him on the shoulder and when he turned, gave him a solid facer, knocking him to the ground. No one paid attention to the downed man.

Clay checked the coat of arms on the carriage door. Yes, it was the Lynford crest. He seemed to remember a story his mother once told him. He might have to pay her a visit for the details. Right now, he had to see to his Nicola.

He hurried to the side of the barn where he had left her. There was no Nicola and no Eel in sight.

I swear that woman is going to drive me...She never, never does what I tell her.

"Eel and Miss Nicola left," Jeb said. "They be going to the Highbridge house. Look what I found in the carriage." He dropped Nicola's healing bag at his feet.

Clay picked up the bag and walked around the barn. He needed to let his temper cool. He needed to think.

I do not need nor want a woman like Nicola in my life. Trouble seems to find her or she finds it. If there is a problem she is right in the middle of it. She is not a proper woman, thinking of marriage, babies and the like. He stopped and laughed out loud. *I don't like proper women. They have no minds of their own.*

Barnaby caught up with Clay. "So what's next? Between our mission and rescuing Miss Highbridge, more than once I might add, we have been very busy."

"I know this all seems strange." Clay frowned and stopped in his tracks. "You see I have become very attracted to Miss Highbridge."

"Tell me something I don't know." Barnaby

laughed. "It might have taken you this long to figure it out. But me, I knew days ago."

****

Mr. Simons and his cart of fresh cut hay dropped Nicola and Eel at the Highbridge home. He promised to deliver a cart of coal to the Smith house anonymously, and to do so for the rest of the year.

Mara, Susan, Aunt Belle, and Emmy greeted Eel and Nicola. All started to talk at the same time.

"Wait." She held up her hand. "First I must have a bath, then something to eat. Then I shall tell you my tale."

She left them standing in the kitchen and went to her room. She paced back and forth trying her best to stay awake. She laid out clean clothes. The tub arrived, she added lavender and rose oil to the steaming water and climbed in. The one time she wanted to sit and soak she couldn't. It would be rude; everyone was waiting for her. She washed and scrubbed herself until she felt and smelled clean.

The sound of voices reached her halfway down the stairs. It appeared like the whole of London was gathered in the house. Nicola opened the kitchen door, not sure she wanted to see anyone, until she smelled the food. She moved into the room. A place had been set at the table. Was it for her? Nicola didn't take a chance and sat down.

People sat around the table all started asking questions at the same time. Nicola ignored them and filled her plate with food from the many dishes.

"I cannot hear if all of you talk at the same time. I would like to be the first to speak, after I have eaten."

It was not long before the only sound in the room

was the silverware clicking on the plates while everyone ate. But Nicola couldn't eat very much despite her hunger.

"I would like to start by thanking everyone looking for me. I am not sure what their plans were but—" Her voice cracked, a large lump formed in her throat, and tears gathered in her eyes.

"We are glad you are home and safe, Sister Dear." Mara touched Nicola's arm with a shaking hand.

"The men who kidnapped you are on their way to Newgate." Clay stood in the doorway. "The Runners will question them. But you need to tell us what happened."

Nicola related the story from the time she left the Smith house. "I have no idea who is responsible for this. Those men were hired thugs and only spoke to threaten me."

"Barnaby and I will be questioning them as well to see what we can discover. Please do not leave the house. The person or persons responsible are still out there somewhere."

She looked up at Clay and opened her mouth. One look at his tired, drawn face and she nodded her head in agreement.

It took every ounce of energy Nicola had left, but she managed to stand and announce. "I am going to bed."

She closed the door behind her, leaned against it, and shut her eyes to gather her strength to climb the stairs.

"You need my help?" Clay touched his lips to her cheek.

He was careful when he lifted Nicola and cradled

her in his arms. She snuggled into him, resting her head on his shoulder, as he climbed the stairs. His breathing was the only sound as he walked down the hallway.

"Please open the door, my dear." He stopped at her bedroom and dipped her down so she could reach the doorknob.

The click of the latch prompted her to push it open with her foot. He surveyed the room as he walked toward her bed. Nicola floated out of her daydream and realized where they were.

"Clay, Mr. Barber, put me down. This is not proper. You must leave at once."

"I know this is not the time or place." He looked into her eyes. "Do not say another word." He sat down on the bed with her in his lap. "I need to tell you—I love you. I was terrified we would never find you. You mean more to me than life itself."

When he kissed her, she closed her eyes and floated into space. She came back to reality when her stomach felt the slam of the heat and need, which grabbed at her. She broke the kiss but the ribbon of current still flowed between their bodies.

"I cannot believe this is happening," she whispered. "I...you must leave. If Aunt Belle should see us..."

"We are meant to be together, my dear. I leave you to rest." He eased her off his lap and pulled the servant bell cord hanging next to the bed.

Sally entered the room and stood wide-eyed as he left. She helped a silent Nicola prepare for bed.

Chapter Twenty-Two

Clay arranged for four Runners to be stationed outside the house. He stood in the darkness waiting for Barnaby. Everyone else had either gone home or retired for the evening.

Two Runners hid in the front yard, in the shadows. Two more were stationed in the back near the main house. One stood in the doorway of the carriage house and one hid in a small outbuilding. They would see if anyone came to the house or if anyone left. Clay arranged for two other Runners to take over during the day. Whoever had kidnapped Nicola might choose to strike again. When Barnaby finally arrived, he and Clay started for home.

"Who do you think is behind this?" Barnaby broke the silence. "I seen the family crest on the carriage. It does not make sense to me."

"Me neither, but the facts are what they are." Clay frowned and sighed. "Why would Malcolm Lynford have any interest in Nicola?" He rubbed the side of his face with his left hand. "Since I saw the signet ring…" He touched his pocket and until that moment he had forgotten he had placed both the earrings and the ring there. "I have seen the ring before. For some reason the griffin is familiar to me. But I cannot remember where—only that I have." Clay stopped.

"Could we keep moving toward home?" Barnaby

asked. "I am tired beyond words, and now I am cold too. Not sleeping does that to me. If you stop too long I may just find a corner to sleep in like in the war."

"Yes, by all means. Let us get you home." He slapped Barnaby on the shoulder. "You do need your beauty rest."

Very funny," Barnaby said, with laughter in his voice. "What do you remember about the signet ring?"

"It has something to do with one of my father's friends, a Duke of… For the life of me I cannot think of the rest of the title," Clay said, with a groan. "I have mislaid the information in my very tired brain."

****

Morning came early for Clay. After a few hours of sleep, he awoke with the missing answer. Nicholas, Duke of Russellton, had been his father's closest friend until the woman the Duke had chosen to marry left, disappeared, or married someone else. He couldn't remember what happened, but it had become the on-dit of the year. Nicholas became a recluse, seeing no one, not even his father.

He remembered the signet ring because as a child he had been fascinated by it. Nicholas had shown him how it worked. In fact, in his rooms at his parents' home, he still had a small box filled with waxed seals they made one rainy afternoon.

He penned a note for Barnaby and placed it on the center of the hall table. Then he left the house and hurried to saddle his horse, Caesar, for the long ride.

****

Nicola lay in bed and remembered Clay's words. He loved her. Her face radiated the happiness she felt from her head to her toes. Before she told him her true feelings she would have to explain about her parents. They had much to discuss.

To her surprise and delight when she looked into the room where Eel had been staying, she found the boy asleep on a make-shift cot and his mother in bed. She didn't want to wake him, but she needed his help in locating Mr. Barber.

Eel's mother woke when Nicola approached the bed.

"Sorry to disturb you, Susan. But I must see Mr. Barber immediately and Eel knows where he resides."

"Wake 'im, miss. He thinks so 'ighly of you 'e would be upset if you did not."

Nicola approached the cot and touched the boy's shoulder. "Eel, wake up," she whispered. He didn't stir, just turned his face away. "It appears he would rather sleep."

"Miss Nicola, you get dressed. I will have 'im up and out of this room in less than ten minutes."

"Thank you. I will meet him in the kitchen. We can get something to eat before we leave."

Eel sat at the kitchen table eating scones and drinking a steaming cup of tea when she walked in. The aroma of fresh baked bread and scones made her stomach growl.

"Good morning, miss," Cook and Eel said together.

"Please 'elp yourself to a fresh scone or some of me bread. There be fresh preserves too." Cook pushed a jar toward her.

"I will have one of those please." She sat next to Eel. "Good morning to you, young man." In a happy mood, she reached over and tousled his hair.

The man she loved, loved her. Fancy that.

"Me mom, I mean my mother," said Eel, "thinks you wants me to escort you to Mr. Barber's house."

"I must speak with him." She washed her hands at the sink, as was her habit. "I am sorry I got you out of bed so early. This cannot wait."

Eel waited until he finished chewing his mouthful of food. "That will be fine."

"You are doing well with your speaking." She smiled. "How are you doing with your writing?"

"I am doing well." Eel laughed. "When I speak proper it sounds strange. Sometimes I want to turn around and see who is talking. Then I realize it is me."

"When we get back"—she stirred cream into her tea—"might you show me your newly acquired penmanship skills?"

"Yes, miss."

They left the house the moment they were finished. It was so cold their breath curled in the air. Both were bundled in a coat, cap, and scarf. Nicola wore her walking boots. She still didn't like walking on the cobbled street even with the heavier soles.

"Eel," she whispered. "Someone is following us."

"It be one of the Runners. Mr. Barber, he hired them to guard you until whoever be responsible for taking you be caught. I know you do not like it."

"I think it is wonderful of Mr. Barber to be concerned about me, us."

"You do not mind?" Eel's eyebrows shot up.

"It was thoughtful and considerate."

Out of habit he led the way to the back entrance and knocked. When no one answered, he beat on the door. Both of them stomped their feet trying to stay warm. He continued to knock, and when his hand got tired, Nicola took over.

The door opened, and Barnaby stood glaring at them.

"What do you want?"

"We…I came to see Mr. Barber," Nicola said.

"Come in. I'll build up the fire in the kitchen stove. It will heat faster than the fireplace in the library. Both of you are turning blue."

They followed him into the small kitchen.

Surely Clay and Barnaby do not live here. Something is—

Barnaby stoked the fire and then said, "I do not understand how Clay managed to sleep through the racket. I'll get dressed and fetch him."

The room had gotten a little warmer by the time Barnaby returned. He carried a paper folded in half in his hand, which he held out to her. She read the note out loud.

"Dear Barnaby,

I remembered what I had forgotten last night. I am going to do some investigating. I will return in two to three days. Carry on. You know what to do.

Clay"

"How could he leave after last night?" Her shoulders slumped, and she sighed.

"He would not have left if it were not important." Barnaby frowned.

"What does he mean 'He remembered what he forgot'?"

"No idea." Barnaby shrugged his shoulders. "I will make sure he comes to see you when he returns."

"Come." She took Eel's hand. "This turned out to be a waste of time and effort."

Her hurried walk back from Clay's house was long and silent. How could she have jumped to such conclusions? He had said the most wonderful thing to her, given her hope, and then left. She sighed. She knew Clay had discovered her lack of family. He had left and would never return.

When Nicola reached home, she immediately went back to bed. She placed the note Clay left for Barnaby under her pillow. After troubled dreams, she finally gave up and dressed for the second time. She put the note inside her bodice next to her breast, close to her heart. She needed to get on with her day. No point in crying over something she had no control over.

She went to find solace in her healing room. But when she opened the door, she found the place filled with people. Eel was not there to organize everyone as he was in school. The room quieted down the moment everyone noticed her standing in the doorway.

There were the usual cuts, bruises and the like. Halfway through the afternoon, she began to long for her quiet cottage in Chew Magna.

Her reason for staying in London had evaporated along with the disappearance of George. She could now return to her dull, boring, yet peaceful existence in her backwater town.

However, there were not many places in London for those who had little or no money to get quality herbal or medical attention. She couldn't leave until she found someone to take over her practice. She couldn't desert the people she had come to care for in such a short time.

Until she left she would continue to look for her parents. It had suddenly become more important to her than anything else in life. Henry, the man she once thought she loved, could not marry her because she didn't know who her parents were. He said he didn't care but his parents did. She would never forget their words.

"My dear, they may well be thieves or cut throats. Our Henry must champion the family name. He cannot and will not marry someone who has no idea who or what her family is."

Nicola had never spoken to Henry again. She had somehow got home that awful day and survived the days which followed. He left to do the grand tour the next morning. When he returned months later, Henry had a wife, a very rich Italian wife.

Nicola, too, had left the next day and vowed never to return until she knew who her parents were.

The days flew by. Clay continued his habit of sneaking into her thoughts. She loved him, without a doubt, but she had loved before and gotten over it. She would this time too.

Chapter Twenty-Three

Clay rode hard. The wind pulled at his clothes. The mist touched his face and froze in place. He rode until he came to The Boar Inn. The coaching yard overflowed with people, laughing, shouting, and talking together. The coaches were lined up, but he paid little attention to them or any of the individuals.

He threw the stable lad a gold coin. "I will be leaving within an hour. Wipe down the horse. Give him water, and grain."

Clay strode into the inn and ordered breakfast with strong tea. An hour later he was back in the saddle. The sun was breaking through the clouds and the mist had disappeared. He was weary from lack of sleep but still determined. He paused at the half rock wall, which graced the entrance to Brookhaven Manor.

Next to each side of the wall sat a regal lion head, on a huge stone block, daring anyone to pass. How frightened he had been as a child when he first saw them. A wooden fence ran from the animal's perch to the woods. The main gate stood open. He rode past it down the long drive, which curved and flowed through the rolling hills. The manor house stood regal in the sun at the end of the long road. The right fork went to the front entrance, while the left fork went around to the lake. Black swans floated on the calm water, creating ripples, which fanned across the water. The beautiful picture hadn't changed in all the years since he had last been there.

He tied his horse to a post close to the massive door. "Don't worry, Caesar. I will see you are rubbed down and given extra grain." He patted his weary horse.

The door opened as he approached. A withered old man stood in the open doorway. "May I assist you, sir?"

He couldn't remember the man's name, but he did recall him. He still looked as old as time.

"I have urgent business with Nicholas Lynford.

"Do you have an appointment, sir?"

"No. I have been on the road since before the sun came up." He pointed to his horse, which stomped its feet. Lather from the hard ride had collected around Caesar's bridle and saddle. "I need someone to care for my horse."

"I will return in a few minutes more or less." The old man turned, shut, and locked the door in his face.

"You know, Caesar,"—he used the scraper to clean his boots lest he fall asleep standing up—"if the man does not hurry I will—"

The door reopened.

"The Duke of Russellton requested your card. He is not available. He will contact you at his earliest convenience."

With a deep sigh, Clay pushed the old man out of the way and barged into the entryway.

"Nicholas, where the hell are you? It is Clay Barber."

Three men came running down the hallway while the butler regained his composure.

"Please, sir, you must leave or we will be forced to

throw you out."

"I think not. You are all welcome to try."

The four servants stood glowering at Clay, who stood with his back against the opened door and watched them form a half circle around him.

I can take them but I'd rather not. They are, after all, old, and small.

Digging in his pocket, Clay pulled out Nicola's signet ring and offered it to the butler. "Give this to Nicholas. I think you will find he will see me."

"Sir, the duke will not see you."

"I know what he said. Now show him the ring."

The butler hurried away and returned quicker than he had left.

"The duke will be here momentarily. Please follow me to the breakfast room."

Clay tried to smile but couldn't. He followed the servant.

He sat and watched the swans glide across the lake. The quiet of the moment and the fact he was sitting still had him dozing off within minutes.

****

Nicholas Lynford, seventh Duke of Russellton, walked through the door and watched his old friend's son sleep. Before he entered, he had made sure the lad's horse had been taken to the stables. The groom confirmed the horse had been ridden hard, very hard.

I wonder what brought him here. I haven't seen or talked to him or his father in years, too many years. Not since she left me. If the situation had been different.

Looking back in time caused him great pain and made him feel far too old. Joy left his life a long time ago. He had known for years he should change, try to find happiness. But over the years, he found he couldn't look to the future because, he couldn't leave the past behind where it belonged.

Nicholas poured a cup of hot chocolate, from the silver pot, on the sideboard. Before taking a sip, he inhaled the aroma of his favorite morning beverage. He strolled around the room and cleared his throat numerous times. Yet Clay slept on. Finally, he tugged the bell pull.

"Bring some food," he said to the maid who entered the room. "I think my young friend will be hungry if he ever wakes up."

The maid curtsied and left.

"I am quite awake," Clay announced the moment the door closed. "How could I not be with all the noise?" He stood, smiled, and shook Nicholas's outstretched hand.

"You have given my household, and especially Wolly, my servant, an unusual start this morning." The duke paused, glancing at Clay's clothes. "I hope the reason you are here was worth your ride, because in truth, young man, you look like hell."

"I will apologize to Wolly later. When I tell you why I am here you will thank me, I hope."

The maid returned pushing a cart laden with food and drink. She arranged fresh bacon, breads, and scrambled eggs on the sideboard and placed a pitcher of chilled apple cider on the table along with tall glasses.

"Would you like me to serve, sir?"

"We will take care of ourselves. We are not to be disturbed by anyone. If we are, I will sack that person without references."

"I be passing the word to Mr. Wolly." She scurried

out of the room without a backward glance.

The men strolled to the window and stood side-by-side enjoying the calm of the lake. The silence was broken when the door shut.

"Now lad, tell me why you have come and how you came by this." He held out the ring in the palm of his hand.

"A most interesting tale, sir." Clay's stomach omitted a large growl. "Will you not join me? It has been a long time since I have eaten." He proceeded to the sideboard, filled his plate, sat at the table, drank his tea, and ate until his plate was clean.

"The ring belongs to a very dear friend. In fact, the woman I plan to marry," Clay admitted. "She received it on her birthday. Her eighteenth birthday. I am not sure where to start because I know only what I believe is the conclusion. I have my suspicions but few facts to base them on."

Nicholas started to speak, tried to clear his throat, coughed, and took a drink of the cider Clay offered him. The lump, however, remained. He found it hard to talk about his one true love of long ago. Finally, he said, "I had this ring, or one like it, made for a young woman. I gave it to her when she agreed to wed me. I had not yet asked her father for her hand. Our agreement was a private promise. Then I found out she loved another. She disappeared, without a word."

"Sir, I believe you were led down the proverbial path."

"You, young man, do not know what utter nonsense you are speaking." The duke stiffened and crossed his arms over his chest

"You might be right. However, let me tell my story

and you fill in any blanks along the way." Clay looked at him until their eyes met. "Do you agree?"

Nicholas nodded his head before he lowered his eyes and stared at the ring in his hand.

"A foster mother raised my future bride," Clay said. "On her eighteenth birthday she received two items belonging to her birth parents." He took the napkin from his lap and set it on the table. "One, the signet ring you hold in your hand."

"The other item?" Nicholas stood so quickly he almost toppled over his chair. "What was it?" His heart beat so hard, he found it difficult to take a deep breath. "Do you have any idea?"

Clay also stood and took a small box from his jacket pocket, opened it, and walked toward him.

"Here is the other item."

"I cannot bear to look." Nicholas appeared to be frozen in place. "Tell me. What is in the box?"

"Please sit down, sir." Clay sat and waited for Nicholas to join him. "The box holds a beautiful pair of amethyst and emerald earrings set in gold. They were a gift from my bride's birth mother.

"She received them on her eighteenth birthday," Nicholas whispered so softly Clay almost couldn't hear him.

"Do you know the rightful owner, sir?"

"Yes, but I do not understand. This means—I have a daughter. Why would my darling leave me if she were going to have our child?" Nicholas blinked back his tears.

"Sir, if you will allow me, I believe I can answer some of your questions." Clay smiled. "Your darling's name is Catherine Highbridge."

Nicholas nodded his head.

"Your brother Malcolm, I believe, is the one who told you she loved another?"

Nicholas stared at Clay, unable to think, unable to answer.

"Am I correct?"

"Yes. What does Malcolm have to do with this?" He slammed his fisted right hand into his opened left hand. Whack, whack, whack.

"I believe when you contact Miss Highbridge you will find Malcolm told her much the same story he told you." Clay paused and rubbed the back of his neck. "My guess is she disappeared with the help of Malcolm."

"I tried to find her. I spent months, contacted everyone who knew her." The duke sighed. The feeling of loss and hopelessness again washed over him. "She disappeared off the face of the earth. Someone said she went to the Colonies."

"You spoke to all these people or did Malcolm?" Clay asked.

"I could not function, my heart broken into pieces." His broad shoulders slumped and he clenched his teeth. "My brother, why would he do such thing? He told me he spoke to everyone, even showed me letters from various people confirming his story." Nicholas gripped the arms of the chair. "Why? I do not understand."

"Sir, I know you have a beautiful daughter." Clay smiled. "Why Malcolm did what he did, I do not know. But I am sure in time we will ferret out the reason for his actions." Clay frowned.

"My daughter," Nicholas prodded. "What is her name?"

"Nicola, her name is Nicola. You and she share the same brilliant blue eyes, square chin, and smiles. She looks a lot like you. Nicola Highbridge is your daughter."

Tears streamed down Nicholas's face.

"I came not to upset you. I came to set a wrong right. I love your daughter. Before we can start a life together, she needs to know her parents. She has so many questions."

Nicholas could not sit still a moment longer. He reached out and pulled Clay to him. "You have my blessing and my—Oh, I have a grown daughter!" He looked out the window while the past fluttered through his mind.

"Her mother must hate me. There are so many questions to be asked and answered. Where is my Catherine? Do you know?"

Nicholas turned back to Clay. He held his breath waiting. He still found it hard to swallow, as the lump in his throat had not budged but grown larger, and his mouth had become drier. He needed to see Catherine. He had to find her. This time he would not let her go.

"I will take you to her because I have some questions of my own only the two of you can answer. She lives in Milborne Port, near Sherborne."

Nicholas flung open the door. "Wolly, where are you? Bring my horse around. Pack a few clothes." He jammed his hands into his pockets. "I will be gone for a week or maybe longer.

Wolly arrived along with the rest of the servants.

"Sir, if you are to be gone for a week it would be best to take your carriage. It will be more comfortable for you."

"It will take too long, to get to—Where are we going? I have forgotten." Nicholas turned to Clay.

"To Milborne Port."

"Get my horse, Wolly. Now." He slapped his hand against his leg to show the urgency of his request. "I also have another task for you to perform."

Nicholas stopped and took a hard look at Clay. No doubt the long hours spent on the ride from London would have Clay's body protesting now or within a short time. His young friend needed rest, and he needed time to think all this through.

"Wolly, wait. We will leave tomorrow at first light. This young man needs to rest. You and I have plans to make. I need to think. Come, Clay, I have a few more questions."

Chapter Twenty-Four

After two days of hard riding, Nicholas and Clay cantered through the gate at Highbridge Manor. They stopped only to refresh their horses and themselves when necessary.

"Young man, should we not send a message requesting a visit, not just appear?"

Clay watched Nicolas run his hand up and down the leg he had hurt in a long ago hunting accident. Even the horse prancing about did not stop his nervous gestures.

"Sir, I must get back to London. I have urgent business for the government. If I had sent a message to you, would you have seen me?"

"I see your point. I am more nervous than when my father took me to his mistress for lessons in lovemaking."

"Your father did what?"

"My father wanted me to know what taking care of basic needs was all about. He did not want me to learn from the dairymaids or a doxy who hoped to trap me into matrimony." He smiled at the memory. "It was an interesting time in my young life."

"One would think so."

They tied their horses to the post to the left of the door. Clay used the brass doorknocker to announce their arrival. A young maid opened the door.

"You be lost?"

"No. We are here to see Miss Catherine Highbridge." Clay clenched his jaw and rubbed his neck.

"Who should I say be calling? That be if she be home."

Clay waited for Nicholas to answer the maid. He said nothing. Just stared straight ahead.

"Sir, your name?"

Clay stood with his arms crossed and walked through the door into the hallway with Nicholas right behind him. The maid hurried away.

"You could have said something," Clay muttered.

"I could not think of anything to say. I was afraid if I opened my mouth the maid would think I sounded like a simpleton."

The maid returned in minutes with an old woman who had keys jiggling from her waist as she approached.

The old woman stopped and stood in their path. Before either of them could utter a word she said, "You have been told Miss Highbridge might not be available. Do you have an appointment? If not, you must leave." She pointed to the door.

"Please." Nicholas took his signet ring off his finger and placed it along with Nicola's ring in the old woman's hand. "Give these to Miss Highbridge. I am sure she will see us."

The old woman looked hard at Nicholas. "Have we met?"

****

Catherine Highbridge looked intently at the rings cradled in her hand. One of them was hers. But no, her ring hung on a gold chain around her neck and lay nestled between her breasts. She never took it off.

It could not be Nicholas's ring. He would never part with it, not even in death. He had told her so many times.

She closed her eyes and smiled sadly as his handsome face filled her mind, even after all these years. She had lost him to another so long ago, yet her eyes still filled with tears over what might have been. She recalled the day her life changed forever. Malcolm had been so kind, helpful, and understanding. He helped her during those dark days when her heart broke into a million pieces.

Her chin trembled, she shook her head, and sighed. There was no way around it. She would have to face those men downstairs. The past was gone, and Catherine had to live in the present.

****

The men waited in the yellow and blue sitting room. The fire in the hearth made the area warm and cozy. The smell of lavender hung in the air. In the corner sat a needlepoint tapestry. Someone was painstakingly crafting a winter scene. Nicholas ran his finger across the smooth edge of the frame holding the cloth in place. Clay stirred the fire and added a new log. The early morning ride had been cold.

The moment the door opened, both men sprang into action. Clay turned to greet Miss Catherine and stared. Nicola didn't look much like her mother but their mannerisms were similar. Nicola carried herself regally like her mother, and their hair color was a close match.

"Young man, I do not believe we have met."

Catherine walked toward him. "I would have remembered you, I am sure."

"We have not had the pleasure of meeting. However, I have met your daughter. While you do not look like her. You are the same." He bowed.

"You mean one of my foster daughters, do you not?"

Nicholas took one large step into the center of the room and interrupted. "My dearest Catherine, I have looked everywhere for you. A day does not go by I do not think about you and miss you."

Catherine spun around. She stood between the two men. Nicholas moved to block the door so she couldn't escape.

"Is it really you? Why are you here?" she whispered. "You are married. Malcolm told me." She placed her hand to her chest. "He swore on my family Bible you…"

Nicholas reached her side and gathered her tightly in his arms.

"Please let me go," she whispered into his ear. "I cannot breathe."

He picked her up and walked to the nearest chair and sat down with her in his lap. Clay walked out of the room, and closed the door.

They talked for hours while Clay stood outside the door and would not let anyone in. Once Catherine assured Birdie, the old woman and housekeeper, no harm had befallen her, a table and chair were brought for his use. Tea, sandwiches, and *The London Times* were delivered by the butler on a silver platter.

Clay intended to stand guard until the door was opened from the inside. But Wolly appeared very late in the afternoon with a special license and the local vicar. Clay knocked on the door when he heard what Nicholas had in mind.

"Sir, Wolly is here with the vicar. May we come in?"

Catherine rushed to the door and opened it with a smile on her face and a sparkle in her eyes. Her radiance made her look much younger.

"Oh dear, I must change. We are to be wed. I must—"

"Let me be the first to congratulate you. I hope in time you will become my mother-in-law." He reached down and kissed both her cheeks.

"Your mother-in-law?"

"We will explain later, my dear." Nicholas stood next to her. "Please go change into your finery. I will not wait for more than one hour, madam."

Catherine conferred with Birdie as they rushed up the stairs. The house hustled and bustled with activity. Stands of flowers were placed in the small ballroom. The room looked like an indoor garden by the time the staff finished.

Catherine and Nicholas were married in a quiet ceremony with Clay and Birdie as witnesses.

****

The next morning Clay, the Duke and Duchess of Russellton enjoyed a quiet breakfast.

"It is time for me to take my leave," Clay announced. "I must return to London." He placed his napkin on the table, stood, and strolled over to the newlyweds.

"How are we ever to thank you for your kindness?" Catherine asked.

209

"Young man, we owe you more than we can repay." Nicholas took his wife's hand and helped her from the table.

"Your husband is aware of my feelings for your daughter." Clay moved toward Catherine. "But, madam, you are not. I love Nicola and plan to ask her to be my wife."

Catherine gathered him in her arms, released him, and took two steps back. "I hope she accepts your offer."

"I must conclude my business in London before I can make plans for the future." Clay paced the room. "I believe Malcolm is one of the ring leaders of the Spenceans."

"I have heard of them." Nicholas followed the man who had changed his life across the floor. "But I thought they were disbanded. Are you sure it is the same group of thugs and ruffians?"

"The one detail I am sure of is Malcolm's involvement."

"I would be remiss if I did not ask if there is some way I can help." Nicholas touched Clay's shoulder. "Do you need money or men?"

"All is under control or as much as can be at the moment." He sighed. "I would like to make a suggestion—your daughter needs to know you are her parents. She needs to hear and understand the entire story from both of you."

"I have wanted to acknowledge her all these years as my true daughter." Her face glowed with pride and happiness.

"She must also leave London. Malcolm kidnapped her once, and I believe she would have come to great

210

harm if we had not found her in time."

"I do not understand why Malcolm would do such an evil thing." Catherine bit her lip and look at the floor. "You have to be mistaken."

"There are many questions only Malcolm can answer. I believe it all somehow comes back to his desire for power and control."

"He has great influence," Nicholas said. "When my dear Catherine disappeared, I became the shell of a man. I let Malcolm manage all the family businesses, while I became the farmer. Hard physical work has kept me going through the years." He stopped near Catherine and gripped the side of the table with such force his knuckles turned white. She reached over and patted his calloused hands. Nicholas smiled at her and continued. "He has added great wealth to our coffers. Malcolm is a forward thinking man, way ahead of his peers. Others have followed many of his concepts. Even the King and Prince Regent look to him on many matters."

"That may be. But remember what he did to the two of you." He touched Nicola's ring, which again lay in his pocket with the earrings. She never strayed from his thoughts. "Malcolm will do whatever it takes to accomplish his plans. Please remember the man is evil to the core."

"I will write to Nicola," Catherine said, "to invite her here. Will you carry the message to her?"

"Duchess—"

"Call me Catherine. After all we are soon to be related." She beamed.

He had to blink twice because his mind visualized his Nicola smiling at him, not her mother.

"I will be delighted to deliver your message and will see she leaves first thing tomorrow morning."

He arrived in London late in the afternoon.

Chapter Twenty-Five

Clay opened the outer door, stood inside, and watched Nicola working at her desk.

"Well, you decided to return." She went back to reading her book, *The Complete Herbal and English Physician Enlarged.*

He walked over, took the book from her hands, and closed it.

"Why you—"

"Still cannot think of a name for me?" He reached down and pulled her up to stand next to him. "Can you?" He gathered her into his arms and hugged her. He relaxed when her arms went around him and returned his embrace. "I have missed you more than I realized was possible." He pulled back to look into her eyes. "You know I love you, with all my heart and soul. Nicola, will you marry me?"

"Will I what?" She blinked.

"Marry me, be my wife and I will be your husband, forever through eternity."

"Clay, I cannot." She tugged away from him and he let her go. "Until I learn my family history, I cannot marry. What if my parents or ancestors were evil people? Many defects can be passed on to children."

"Nicola, in God's name what are you talking about?" He wanted to shake her. She didn't make any sense.

"Your parents would never approve of me. They would forbid you to marry me. "

"My parents would do no such thing. Could it be you do not love me?" He put his hands in his pockets.

"You silly man, of course, I love you with all my heart." She shuttered and smoothed her dress. "I have been through this before." Without looking up, she explained about Henry and his mother's cruel words.

"The man was a fool of the first order and probably still is. If I ever find him I will give him a good measure of one of Gentlemen Jim's facers, which will have him seeing stars for a week."

When she started to cry, he kissed her tears away.

"I have a message for you." He handed her the note, then settled himself in the chair to watch her reaction.

Nicola tore at the envelope and with great care placed it on the desk. She grasped the folded stationery in her hand. "How did you get a message from Catherine and why would you hand carry it to me?"

"Read it my dear and it will become clear."

She opened up the folded piece of paper.
"My Dearest Nicola,

I know how important it is for you to find your birth parents. They are waiting to receive you here at Highbridge Manor. Clay will arrange for a carriage to bring you home. We await your arrival.

Love, Catherine"

"I do not understand. My parents are waiting for me?" Nicola stood and placed her hands on her hips. She didn't want to sound rude but felt confused and angry at his knowledge. "How did you get involved in all of this?" It was important she remain in control.

"When you disappeared, I discovered you were searching for your parents and these two items were your only clues to their identities." From his pocket he moved her earrings, ring, and handed them to her. "I believe they had something to do with your disappearance." He reached for the ring and held it up. "I recognized the signet ring, or at least I thought I did. I traveled to confront the man I believed to be your father."

Nicola sat down with a thud.

Oh, I have so many questions, need so many answers. I can't wait.

"Why did you not come and take me to my father?"

"At the time I could not be sure and did not want to give you false hope. You could not travel without a chaperone and a carriage." He yawned and rubbed his freshly shaved chin. "There was not enough time. I still have urgent business here in London."

He again reached for her and gathered her in his arms.

"Oh, how do I thank you?" She surrendered to his warmth, his touch, and rested her head on his chest.

"Agree to be my wife."

"I am going to meet my parents," she shouted, ignoring his proposal. If Clay had not been present, she would have jumped up and down like a child. "Now I will learn why they gave me away like a fresh loaf of bread. What if they do not like me?" She wandered from place to place. "I must pack my bags. Should I pack a trunk? Oh, I must leave now, right this minute. I must—"

"Wait." Clay stopped her by pulling her back into

his arms. "Your carriage will be here tomorrow at dawn to take you to Highbridge Manor. I have arranged it."

She pushed him away and turned to the door. "Why must I wait?'

"The roads are not safe to travel at night." He walked up behind her.

She stopped and he almost ran into her. "But the morning is so long from now." She turned to face him. "I cannot sit here and wait and wait."

"Yes you can, dearest." He once again gathered her into his arms and gave her a kiss that tingled all the way to her toes.

****

Nicola woke long before daylight. The early morning sky was growing lighter when she finally jumped out of bed. She lit candles in her room to verify that both her travel and herbal healing bags were still where she had placed them the night before.

It had taken her a long time to fall asleep. *What if my parents don't like me, want me or—?* Her mind continued to fabricate happy, sad, or angry reunions.

She dressed as fast as she could and sat in the chair in her room waiting and waiting for the sounds of a carriage. She was exhausted from worry and apprehension to the point that the early morning hour lulled her to sleep.

Sally knocked and entered. "Miss, Mr. Barber be here."

Nicola opened her eyes, blinked twice and stood with such speed she needed to grab the table next to her chair to steady herself.

"You be all right?" Sally darted closer.

"I am fine, just a little anxious. I moved too fast."

Nicola draped her woolen cape over her shoulders and fastened the gold clip in place.

Sally picked up Nicola's bags and followed her down the hall. Clay waited at the bottom of the stairs.

"I see you did not sleep well." He caressed her face.

"I did not sleep much. I am too excited, nervous, and anxious all at the same time. Oh Clay, what if they do not like me or want me again?"

"My dearest, believe me when I say you are loved by them and, of course, me. We all want you."

"You are coming with me?" She turned to face him and noticed his frown. "You are not coming, are you?"

"No I must stay here. Sally will travel with you. I have urgent business which must be dealt with."

Clay went to hug her, but she scampered out of his way. She wasn't sure she could face her parents without him at her side. She wanted him, no, she needed him to come with her. Didn't he see how indispensable he was to her? Nicola quickly hopped into the carriage before he could realize her feelings.

"My dear, please understand." He stuck his head in the carriage door. "I must stay. I have a mission I must complete. It is very important to our country."

"I am not sure I care to understand your reasons for staying in London, while I go to meet my parents for the first time. I am sorry I am not important enough."

"Oh please, forgo the melodramatics. You could wait until my business is ended."

"Thank you, no. I have been waiting all my life for this day. I will not waste another minute. Good day, Mr. Barber."

Clay stepped back to assist Sally into the carriage.

Although Nicola tried her best to slam the carriage door, Clay smirked when it only closed politely.

Chapter Twenty-Six

Nicola propped her herbal bag against the carriage window and rested her head against the supple red leather. The fragrances of lavender floated from the bag and soothed her nerves. She fell into a restful sleep. Two hours into the trip she woke refreshed.

"Oh, miss. I ain't never been in the country," Sally said. "It be beautiful."

"Wait until you see Highbridge Manor. The gardens are the finest in the district."

The carriage stopped at the Red Fox Coaching Inn for the horses to be rested and fed. A need to find the necessary had Nicola and Sally leaving the carriage the instant it came to a complete stop. While the horses were watered and fed a small amount of grain, the travelers enjoyed a hasty midday meal. Nicola refused to tarry any longer than necessary and hurried everyone along. They were back on the road in near record time.

They arrived at their destination in the late afternoon. One of the outriggers leaped down and managed to open the carriage door before Nicola could jump out. She all but ran to the house. Sally trudged behind her.

"Miss, we be so delighted to see you," Birdie smiled, as she opened the door.

"It is wonderful to be home. How is Miss Catherine?"

"Not for me to be a-telling you, child," Birdie said "You best go into the sitting room. I will fetch the— Miss Catherine has been waiting for you."

Nicola left her herbal bag on the hall bench with her cape draped over it. Someone would put them away they always did. She strolled to her favorite place in the entire house—the blue and yellow sitting room. She used to curl up with a book there and read for hours or sometimes take an afternoon nap. The cover on the settee looked new. She would wager it was still the most comfortable piece of furniture in the house and it wasn't green.

Nicola stood in front of the fire enjoying the warmth. She wasn't afraid but very, very nervous. Why had Birdie been acting so strangely? The old woman had never been cheerful. Never before could she remember her smiling.

Catherine entered the room and Nicola turned to greet her.

"I am so happy to see you." Nicola rushed to kiss her cheek. "Clay, I mean Mr. Barber, told me you have wonderful news about my parents."

"Yes, I do. First, let us sit and have tea." The clickety-clack of metal wheels on the tile floor announced the arrival of the teacart.

"You still use the old tea cart, I hear?"

"We do. I cannot seem to get rid of it. Every time I try, Birdie rescues it." Catherine walked over to the grouping of chairs and sat down. "Last month I gave it to a peddler. But Birdie found him and bought it back with house money. So it is back to stay. It costs too much to dispose of it." Catherine laughed.

"Your message said my parents were here? Please,

can I meet them? Now?"

Before I lose my nerve.

A tall distinguished man pushed the cart into the room. He looked familiar, but Nicola couldn't remember when she had met or seen him. He stopped beside them.

"My dears, let us have our tea here. Catherine will you pour?" He sat in the chair next to her foster mother.

Catherine didn't say a word but nodded her head in agreement. Nicola observed the amused and delighted glances which passed between them.

"Please sit." He indicated a vacant chair.

Catherine and the man were holding hands. Shocked, Nicola raised her eyebrows.

"How would you like your tea, dear?" Catherine asked.

"I really do not want any refreshment. I would like some answers."

A strange look passed between Catherine and the man.

"Please," Nicola added, remembering her manners.

"And you shall have them, daughter of mine." Catherine set down the teapot.

Nicola jerked up her head and stared into Catherine's emotion-filled eyes. She watched as her foster mother dabbed tears away with her napkin.

"I do not understand. Please do not cry. Sir, might you explain to me? Have my parents decided not to meet me?" Her eyes never left Catherine's face, not for one minute.

"My name is Nicholas Lynford." The man's throat sounded choked with emotion and it seemed he could only whisper. "Catherine and I met many years ago. We loved each other then and still do." He paused, his voice quivering as he took a deep breath. "My brother drove us apart for reasons known only to him." He shook his head. "Your Mr. Barber plans on finding answers for his wicked behavior."

"Are you trying to tell me you are my father?" She finally looked at the man. "I saw your portrait at Malcolm's ball last week." Before he could speak, she raised her hands to stop him. She again looked at Catherine, closer than she had ever looked at her in her life. "Catherine is my real mother?"

The room was silent for a moment.

"Pray tell me. I have it right?"

"Yes my dear daughter, you are correct," Catherine whispered.

Nicola had to strain to hear her.

"Nicholas did not know about you until Mr. Barber showed him your ring." Catherine again dabbed at her eyes with her napkin. "Your Mr. Barber remembered stories from long ago and somehow pieced the story together. The fact your Uncle Malcolm might have kidnapped you is the only reason your father and I are together now. Your Mr. Barber—"

"Do not call him *my* Mr. Barber," Nicola cut in sharply. She jumped up and stood with her hands on her hips. "To think, he knew all this and did not bother to tell me. I do not know what I will do to him when I see him."

She dropped back into the chair, her eyes closed. The humming in her ears blocked out her parents' voices.

My parents. I have found my parents. No, they have found me. No, Clay found them. They are sitting right in front of me. I could be angry, storm, shout, and make everyone unhappy but…I have my parents. I have my family. I know where I came from and where I belong.

She bowed her head and offered a silent prayer. Then she opened her eyes and jumped up once again.

"I have my parents," she shouted. "Finally after all this time I have my family." She moved quickly around the table. She reached Catherine first and hugged her. "Mother, what a wonderful word to be able to say to you. I am so very, very pleased`it is you." A hand touched her shoulder and she turned into her father's arms. "Oh, Father, I am so happy to have you too."

The three stood there for some time. Catherine put her arms around both Nicholas and Nicola. Tears glistened on all their faces but no one cared.

"Dear daughter, we do have more to tell you," Nicholas said. "You are so like your mother. But you do look more like me which pleases me very much." Taking her face in both of his hands, he peered into her eyes washed with tears. "I am not sure you got the best of the bargain, however." He reached out and kissed her on both tear-stained cheeks.

"Sir, I mean Father, I have so many questions about our family. We are a family now. Are we not?"

"Yes, daughter, we are." Catherine laughed. "We have much to talk about."

"I would like to introduce you to my wife." Nicholas took Catherine's hand. "The Duchess of Russellton."

"Oh my." Nicola sat down in her mother's chair.

Nicholas told the story of Malcolm's betrayal, Clay's wild ride to his estate, then their journey to confront Catherine, and his determination to marry the love of his life.

"So you see, my dear, we were married two days ago. We should have waited for you perhaps. However, I feared something would once again prevent our marriage so…"

Nicola couldn't have been happier and beamed approval. Although a little disappointed she had missed the event, she truly understood.

"We need champagne to celebrate my newfound family and the marriage of my parents. Better late than never." Nicola went to the bell pull and gave it a hard couple of tugs.

They toasted each other until the bottles ran dry.

****

Nicola stood in her favorite place on the Highbridge estate, the picture-perfect botanical gardens. She always wished her talents lay in painting. But no matter how hard she tried she couldn't paint worth a hoot.

She had just spent the most wonderful five days in her entire life with her parents—her family. What a joy it was to speak those words. The newly-weds were so delightful, with the hand holding, and the glances they gave each other when they thought no one was looking

But it was time for Nicola to leave. Her parents had a wonderful love to rediscover, and they did not need her around. Now that she had found them, she could depart. They would not disappear. She could come and see them whenever she chose. Besides she had unfinished business with her Mr. Barber.

Nicola could not pinpoint the exact moment her world changed directions. She didn't look different on the outside or inside, but her mind, her reasoning, and her heart had certainly diverted from their original course.

Finding her parents had not made her a whole person. They were important to her. After all, she had hoped to find them her entire life. But the love she felt for Clay Barber was the sunshine which warmed her body and gave her purpose.

She couldn't wait to find Clay and tell him…what? He knew she loved him and the story of her parents was yesterday's news. She smiled. Now, she was finally free to make a commitment. His family couldn't object to his marriage to her. After all, she was the daughter of a duke. Nonetheless, she frowned and chewed on her fingernails.

He was bossy, secretive, and oh, so, handsome. She loved him but… A sigh escaped her lips.

"Something be wrong?" Sally asked. The concern in her voice was unmistakable.

"Everything is fine. I am just"—she sighed again—"just overwhelmed at the moment."

Her father's carriage delivered her to the front door of Aunt Belle's house. She had promised her parents not to say a word until they could make a formal announcement in *The Times*. They wanted to tell Mara and Emmy when they arrived in a few days. It would be hard to keep such a wonderful secret.

A big gala ball was to be planned to introduce the newly married couple and their grown daughter. Nicola wasn't sure the *Ton* would recover from such a shock. But she really didn't care. It would be the talk of this season, and many more to come.

Nicola arrived in London in the late evening, which pleased her. She didn't have to explain her arrival in so fine a carriage, because her sisters and Aunt Belle were at another party. Since they had attended the Lynford Winter Ball, invitations had appeared regularly. She went straight to bed, falling asleep the moment her head touched the pillow.

****

"Nicola, Sister Dear, wake up. Please. I must talk to you. It is very important."

She focused her eyes on Mara sitting on the edge of the bed.

"You will never guess what happened. I overheard two women at Mrs. Pearly's party tonight." Mara again shook Nicola as her eyes closed.

"Pray continue talking and quit shaking me. I am awake."

"I heard one say, 'Dearest Sophia, my mother was correct. Miss Mara Highbridge looks remarkably like her mother'. By the time I got around the row of potted trees, the women had vanished into the crowd. Well, what do you think?"

"Ask me tomorrow." Nicola turned her back to Mara and immediately fell back a sleep.

Chapter Twenty-Seven

"You be sure? Tonight be the night?" Eel asked.

"Yes boy, the entire British cabinet are to be murdered at a meeting in Lord Harrowby's house on Grosvenor Square," Ruthven said.

Ruthven, a Bow Street Runner and former spy, who knew most of the Spenceans, watched the small two-story building on Cato Street along with Barnaby and Eel.

The Spenceans rented the building for weapon storage and as an out-of-the-way place to gather. An ideal location, it suited their needs. The ground floor housed a rundown stable and the second floor a modified hayloft.

Booker, much to Clay's dismay, was to orchestrate the apprehension of the Spenceans, the Cato Conspirators. Booker had instructions from Lord Sidmouth, the Home Secretary, to use men from the Second Battalion Coldstream Guards and the Bow Street Runners to arrest the plotters.

It had been Clay's mission to identify the leaders, and in the process, he uncovered their destructive plans for the evening. His evidence incriminated two men as the string pullers. He wanted them arrested at the scene so there would be no doubt of their involvement.

His instructions, from KM6, were to be on hand to offer his assistance, but only if necessary. His identity was to remain a guarded secret by all involved.

"You must wait for the King's Guards and Clay Barber." Barnaby stood toe to toe with Booker. "You do not understand the power of these people. We need to apprehend the leaders. If we do not, it will only postpone their dastardly deeds for another time. They must be stopped once and for all."

"I do not care about this Clay person or the Guard," Booker shot back. "I be in charge. We be doing what I says."

Booker rocked back and forth on his feet relaying instructions, adding his own terse commands to the Runners who stood behind him. He ignored Barnaby. When a gentlemen's carriage arrived, Booker, too far away to see the passengers, thought it would be a great feat to take them all at once.

Barnaby sent Eel to find Clay and the King's Guards. "Tell Clay to hasten their arrival. All hell is going to break loose. Booker will not listen to me or Ruthven."

Booker believed he had enough men to capture the conspirators and refused to wait. He hid behind an abandoned carriage on the street, while Ruthven led the men up the stairs. They sealed off the ground floor exits and entrance, then burst through the door of the room.

"We are peace officers," shouted Ruthven. "Lay down your arms."

Eel and Clay left the King's Guards when they refused to break formation and hurry to Cato Street. They reached the building as the shots rang out.

The pair approached the building with caution. The street in front looked deserted. Booker came out from behind his hiding place and tried to prevent Clay from entering.

"You are not to enter. I am—"

"I am Clay Barber and you are a fool of the first order." He motioned to two Guards, who had caught up to him. "Do not let this man out of your sight and keep him below stairs."

Booker started to speak until Clay took a step toward him. Booker rubbed his jaw and hurried to hide behind the carriage out of harm's way with the Guards right behind him.

Clay ran up the wooden steps into the loft. The shooting and the clashing of swords had ceased. Angry voices still rang out. He stood in the doorway and dodged to one side, as a man of color tumbled down the stairs headfirst.

"Eel, stay downstairs and guard this man."

Eel pulled a piece of rope out of his pocket and tied him up.

Clay advanced into the room, dodging this way and that, trying his best to stay out of the fist fight. But he managed to land a few punches while he tried to find his quarry.

Clay and Barnaby had been privy to some drawings of the building supplied by a spy in the organization. The original large loft had in recent days been divided into three, a bigger room in the center and two smaller ones. The doors of the smaller areas were closed. Straight ahead stood an open window with a rope ladder secured to its sash. He ran to the opening and watched as two men, gentlemen by the cut of their clothing, ran from the back of the building toward a carriage. The room was in semi-darkness. The smell of gunpowder, sweat of unwashed men, fear and death flowed over him.

Sheer numbers ended the fight. The Runners and the Guards overpowered the Spenceans. Bow Street lost one man, Richard Smithers, and several were wounded. Muffled cries of pain and anger followed Clay as he walked among the men.

"The flock is captured." Barnaby walked up behind him. "Let's hope this will weaken their plans, at least for a while."

"Yes, unless they can gather another group of ruffians quickly. We cannot arrest someone without proper evidence." Anger flowed heavy into Clay's words.

"We did try to stop Booker. He reminded us every chance he got he was in charge. How do people like him get the positions they do?" Barnaby shook his head in disgust.

"Silence. I need some information." Clay moved into the center of the room to talk to the arrested men. "I cannot promise you leniency. I will let the courts know you offered up assistance to prevent killing of innocent people."

"We know nothin'," shouted one brawny man. His hands were tied behind his back, blood ran down the side of his face. He glowered and glanced around the room. "Iffin' you all knows what's good fer you. You be keeping your mouths shut tighter than a—"

Barnaby walked over and stuffed a blood soaked rag in the man's mouth. Ruthven, wounded in the leg, hobbled down the stairs. He too, muttered obscenities about Booker's stupidity.

Clay instructed the Runners to move all the prisoners out of the room and load them into the wagons to take them to Newgate. He made sure the man who had threatened everyone left first. Some of these men were bound to talk but not in front of the others.

"I think I found the man who will help us." Barnaby motioned for Clay to follow him.

They waited for all the prisoners to leave, then walked into one of the smaller rooms. Perched on a makeshift cot sat a small man. He continued to pluck at his blood-stained shirt with one hand, while he held his broken glasses in the other.

"His name be Charles Markers." Barnaby closed the door.

"I understand you can and will provide us with information." Clay sat next to him.

"I can." He slid further away from Clay. His face white from fear, Markers pinched his nose with his thumb and forefinger. He then rubbed his finger under his nose. "You see, I did not want to become involved. I be a humble boot-maker. It be—"

"Did you not have a shop down the road?" Clay asked.

"A good shop, until it burned down. The fire was set, but I could never prove it. These men came to me promising this building, if I did some work for them. I should have known." The small man rubbed his eyes. "What do you want to know?"

"Who are the men in charge?" Clay stood and strolled to the small window. "These thugs on their way to Newgate are just followers. I need to know who leads them."

"What be in it for me to give up their names?" Charles Markers struggled to sit still but kept moving first one leg, then the other, and then his arms.

"I cannot make promises." Clay walked back toward the cot. "But I will offer testimony you volunteered information." He pulled a chair over and sat in front of the man.

"That would get me a knife in my back one dark night in prison. No thanks." The man stood. "I have a family who will never survive by themselves." He pushed past Clay and made for the door.

"Do you think I am daft?" Clay motioned for Barnaby to stand in front of the door. "My plan is to talk to the judge privately and tell him of your support. It will be up to the judge to decide your fate."

"I do not have much of a choice, do I?" Markers walked back, stopped, and stood an even distance between Clay and Barnaby. "If you tell anyone where you got this evidence—"

"You have my word," Clay closed the distance between them. "As a gentleman and my partner's word as—what are you Barnaby?"

"I be a reformed thief, one of the best from the East End." Barnaby moved away from the door.

My word and my partner's word as men of England. No one will know." He offered his hand to the man.

The three shook hands. Leaving two hours later, Clay and Barnaby had the information they needed. Charles Markers produced written documents regarding the group's activity. He was more than a boot maker, he was the organization's accountant. Behind a moveable panel in the wall was all the evidence needed to link Malcolm to the Spenceans.

"If there is a way we can repay you for your help

this day, contact me at the address on this card or through my solicitor. His name is written on the back." Folded behind the card was enough money to give his informant a new start in life.

"Why are you doing this?"

"I believe you were set up and doing the best you could do. Everyone deserves a new start. Use it wisely."

Eel pushed away from the front of the building as soon as he saw Clay and Barnaby leave. He didn't see Charles exit from the side door. The three of them went to the Horse and Groom to eat. Eel left after a hearty meal. Clay and Barnaby took all the papers to their house to review and found details to lead them to where Malcolm and his partner might be hiding.

"We still have no idea why Malcolm is involved, just that he is." Barnaby scratched his head.

They knew Arthur Thistlewood, a known follower of Thomas Spence, preached violent revolution that he believed would solve all of England's problems. The Spenceans believed the killings would create an armed uprising, which would overthrow the current government. A new and improved leadership for England could then be created based on the ideas of the Spenceans. What Thistlewood believed was common knowledge. But Clay was positive Malcolm had his own agenda.

"It does not make any sense." Clay shrugged his shoulders "I can understand Thistlewood but Malcolm? What could he have gained with such a devilish plan?"

****

The London Times
Thursday, February 24, 1820, 3 a.m.
Horrible Conspiracy

We stop the press to publish the following intelligence, which has just reached us.

"A handsome reward of one thousand pounds is hereby offered to any person or persons who shall discover and apprehend, or cause to be discovered or apprehended the said Arthur Thistlewood and Malcolm Lynford."

The article went on to describe both men in detail. A witness declared Thistlewood had been the person responsible for killing of Richard Smithers. Thistlewood stabbed him with his sword.

****

At daybreak Clay and Barnaby met the Bow Street Runners at their office to make plans to find and arrest the wanted men. They sectioned off the city. The reward offered was too great for people to ignore for long. In pairs they went through London looking for the Spenceans' leaders. They posted reward posters on buildings and gave them to everyone they met. It would simply be a matter of time before the money would loosen someone's tongue. Clay and Barnaby's section was the East End, which pleased Barnaby. In his days as a renowned thief, he made the East End his home. He knew places no one else knew of at least not honest folk. They were leaving to begin their search when Eel ran to them with latest addition of *The Times* in his hand.

Second Edition
Thistlewood Apprehended
Half past 12 o'clock.

"We stop the press to announce so satisfactory a piece of intelligence as the apprehension of this daring and atrocious criminal. He was apprehended at 10

minutes before 12, at No. 8, White-Street, Little Moorfields by Vickery and a party from Bow Street."

Barnaby slapped Clay on the back.

"One down, one to go."

Chapter Twenty-Eight

Nicola woke early. She was ready to face the day and had to speak to Clay. She had no idea where to locate him, but she was sure Eel would know. She left the house before anyone else was awake. However, she did not know the school timetable since it had moved and she was no longer involved with its day-to-day operation.

She hurried to Mara's dress shop. Susan and a man were in deep discussion and did not notice her arrival.

Was this the same man who had been arguing with Susan the day she first met her?

"Oh, Miss Nicola, sorry I did not see you." Susan jumped up from the chair. "Can I be of 'elp?"

"I am looking for Eel. Do you know where I might find him?"

"He is out back with Jimmy and Jeb," Susan said.

"Out back?"

Susan pointed to the back of the shop. "The old stable behind Creations. We are not supposed to know Jeb and Jimmy live there, but we do. The lads are doing their schoolwork."

Nicola had no trouble finding the building, which looked like it would fall down at any moment. The weathered and discolored wood gave it an air of mystery.

She knocked on the door. It opened inch by inch

until finally Jeb's face appeared.

"Miss Nicola, please do come in."

The lads were crowded around an old table, a lantern in the middle, using slates to do their schoolwork.

"Good morning to the three of you. I see you are studying. I am so proud of you all."

"How did you know we be 'ere?" Jimmy asked.

"'Here', not 'ere'." She waited for all three boys to say it correctly.

"Your living arrangements are not as secret as you seem to think," Nicola said. "Eel's mother told me where to find you."

"Everyone knows?" Jeb looked puzzled.

"Well Eel's mother, I suspect Mara, and now I know," she said. "So it is not everyone. Eel, I need to talk to you about Mr. Barber. Could we talk outside?"

Eel stood. "I get me coat." He shook his head. "I will get my coat.

They went outside.

"You missed all the excitement. Mr. Barber, he and Barnaby be working for the government and be heroes."

"Clay, I mean Mr. Barber, is not hurt?" Nicola grabbed his arm. "He is—"

"Mr. Barber be fine last time I saw him."

"That is wonderful, Eel." She sighed. "I need to speak to him. Do you know where he is?"

"In the East End looking for the last leader of the Spenceans. Does you want me to 'elp, help, you find him?"

"It is more important you do your schoolwork. I can find Mr. Barber."

Nicola discovered carriage drivers did not want to go to the East End. It took her almost one hour to find a driver, and he only agreed because she offered to pay him double the fare.

She had to find Clay. There was so much to tell him. The driver drove around for an hour as she peered out of the window looking. Finally she had the driver stop.

"Missy, you sure you wants me to leave you. It be not safe here."

"I have to find a friend, a very special one. Meet me back here in an hour. Will you do that?"

"Iffin' you pay me now."

"Do I look lacking? I will pay you double when you return. You get no money from me now." She walked away from the carriage.

People encrusted with dirt and grime stood in the doorways. The smell of food cooking hung in the air along with the stench of rotting flesh. Voices, angry and shrill, carried on the wind which whipped around the buildings. Footsteps echoed behind making her walk faster.

Clay and Barnaby were walking down a deserted street in the East End, checking out the buildings. She supposed they hoped to find any member of the Spenceans who might be able to lead them to Malcolm.

"Clay, Clay Barber," she called out.

Both men turned at her summons. She lifted her skirt and began to run. Clay, too began to move toward her. Suddenly, Nicola felt herself pulled into one of the buildings.

It took her a few seconds to realize what had happened. She fell to her knees. Then against her will, she was jerked to her feet.

The buildings in the area had been warehouses but were falling down from neglect. There were not many windows or doors in place. Most were wrecked, and the walls were crumbling.

"Come along now. You have ruined all my plans, and you're going to pay for your interference."

The darkness kept her captor's face covered but she recognized his voice.

"Uncle Malcolm?"

"Do not call me uncle. Your parents are not married. You were born on the other side of the blanket, the wrong side. I do not recognize you as any part of my family. You are nothing but a she-bastard."

"Where are we going?" she asked.

"Where? I have not decided what to do with you. My mind is too befuddled. I am much too confused at the moment to make decisions."

Malcolm continued to pull her further into the building, which had lost most of its inner walls. The floor was littered with rubble. He moved quickly, picking his way through the maze of debris. Nicola had a hard time keeping up. Her skirt continued to tangle around her feet.

"Wait, they are married now," she called out to her uncle.

"Who is married?" Malcolm growled. "You silly chit." He turned and slapped her across the face. She staggered but he held on. "You are lying. My brother is broken-hearted because Catherine left him. He never leaves Brookhaven. Not once has he left since Catherine disappeared."

"You are wrong, uncle." She felt something

239

crawling on her cheek and brushed it away. "My father found out about my mother and me days ago. They are on their way to London to open the house and announce their marriage and me to the world."

Patches of light filtered through an opening which once held a window. The fine corpulent gentleman was long gone. Malcolm's clothes were filthy, and his hair stood on end. He had not shaved in days. He looked like a beggar and smelled like yesterday's garbage.

"You ruined all my plans, gel."

"How could I have done such a thing? Pray tell."

"You came to London and in time my brother would have heard of you." He massaged his temples, muttered, and shook his head. He stood straight as he could and puffed out his chest. "I am a powerful man because my brother leaves everything to me. He is the farmer, and I am the genius." He pointed a dirty finger at himself. "I will be England's savior. I have friends in the highest of places."

"Whatever does that have to do with me?"

"I planned to kill the British cabinet."

"All of them?" she could not keep the surprise from her voice.

"The whole bloody lot." He stared off into space. "Then I could step in and take control. The King cannot rule, and his son spends money faster than it comes in, believe me. If I took over, I'd make England powerful again." His voice cracked with emotion. "We would return to the colonies and take back what is ours. America belongs to us, the British Empire. Do you not see the right of it?"

"Uncle, I still do not understand what this has to do with me."

He moved to within inches of her face, eyes glaring with malice and pulled her further along into the murky recesses of the building.

Chapter Twenty-Nine

Clay and Barnaby moved into the darkened building.

"I thought I was seeing things," Clay said.

"Ain't this the area they're blasting today?"

Clay and Barnaby waited for their eyes to adjust to the dark. People left their garbage and anything else they were discarding inside the building. Furniture and clothes littered the ground. They didn't stop to look at the rubbish. Shadows of people moved in the distance.

"That way," a voice said. "They be 'eading to the Thames."

The men could now see Malcolm dragging Nicola behind him and hear a smattering of words.

Once again Nicola disappeared from view. Clay quickened his pace, and for once Barnaby was right behind him.

"Do not worry Clay. We will find her."

"It is not the finding I am worried about. It is if she will be alive." He reached for the gun in his pocket. "The man is a lunatic."

"You know who he is?"

"Yes, her damn uncle."

****

Nicola wrinkled her nose at the smell of dirty, infested water before she heard it splash against a nearby dock. She stamped her feet and heard rodents scurry away. Malcolm stood still as a statue.

"I loved Catherine before my brother knew she existed." With a catch in his voice he added, "I still love her. In my heart and mind I knew she belonged to me and me alone." He swiped his hand across his face to cover the tears. "When my brother came to me with their joyful plans to wed, I stopped them." With a sneer on his lips he said, "It did not take much. They both trusted me."

"I know." Nicola bit her bottom lip, thinking of her parents. "They told me the dreadful stories of how you lied to them." Her fear grew, yet she continued, "You should be ashamed. They love each other."

"When she would not have me, I orchestrated it so my brother could not have her either. I did not know about you." He squeezed her arm and continued to drag her along.

"Uncle, you are hurting me," she said, as numbness increased in her arm.

"I established a home for her at the abandoned manor house." Malcolm stopped and glared in Nicola's direction. "I gave her the money to restore it. I have been sending her money for years." He shifted his weight and released her arm. "I saw no reason to visit her. I knew she raised three children but never did I think one would be my niece. A peddler who visited her once a year, was more than happy to keep me informed for a price." He shook his head and tried to smile. "Catherine is smarter than I imagined. Women are not to be trusted." He sneered at Nicola and pinched her hand.

"How did you find out about me?" She rubbed her hand and scowled at him.

"The man in the museum told me about your ring." He dropped his shoulders and sighed. "He recognized the griffin. He overheard you telling the lad about it." Malcolm rubbed his hands together. "He did not understand the importance, but he knew I would."

"You?" Nicola lifted her head and flinched. "You are responsible for the thievery at the museum?" A shiver ran up her spine. "George, the vile man who threatened Emmy, works for you?" She shook her head in disbelief.

"I needed money, hordes of it to buy my way into the Spenceans." He shrugged, and his face again held a vacant expression. "I had the museum pieces stolen and sold them to private collectors throughout the world. The Spenceans are fools. They needed money and did not care where it came from. I needed a group like theirs to cover my true intentions. By the by, George is no more."

"Uncle how could you…?"

"It was with great satisfaction your dear Dr. Cooper breathed his last breath when my knife found its way deep into his heart. It gave me pleasure to watch his body dip and weave as it floated down the Thames before it sank. Peter over the years not only became an incompetent doctor but bungling spy as well. I should have killed Eel and the Rantipoles when I had the chance. After all, you killed my mistress. She was the nimblest thief on my lot."

Nicola started to cry at the shocking news.

"Be still, gel. I am not through." He straightened his posture and tried to smooth his clothes. "People like the Spenceans never look beyond the money. They see what they want to see." He brushed dirt from the front of his jacket, took her arm again, and pulled her toward the outer door and the Thames.

She was so interested in the story unfolding that she almost forgot where she was—in the depths of the very back streets of London's East End. Occasionally, she saw or heard someone moving about, and several times rats bigger than the cats at home ran by.

"Do you not realize your plans are over? Mr. Barber and Bow Street Runners are out looking for you. You know they will find you sooner or later." A shaft of light came through another broken window.

"We'll take my hidden money and disappear. If you do what I say, you will live. If not, one more killing—" He shrugged his shoulders and pursed his lips. "I think you understand, my dear niece."

"Why take me with you?" Nicola asked.

"It is either come with me or I kill you, and throw your body into the Thames."

"You cannot mean—"

Malcom closed his eyes and placed his hands over his ears and began to hum.

"Uncle, you are wrong." Tears ran down her face. She didn't try to stop them. She wasn't sure if the tears were for her, her parents or Malcolm. "We are family. We will support you all we can."

"I understand what will happen to me if I surrender to Bow Street. Everyone will believe I belong in an asylum or worse. I am doomed if I stay in England." He stood in silence for a long time. "My plans for my country are so righteous. Our king cannot rule. His son is not much better. Someone needs to take a hand or this wonderful nation will perish. Do you not see?"

"What I see is a man who cares very much for his

country." She moved closer, reached out, and touched his arm. "Causing people's deaths is not the way."

"One must do what one must do, my dear gel." He shrugged off her touch.

"Oh, uncle, please come with me. I will help you. You are now part of my family. I never knew I had a real family. Please, uncle."

"I planned to kill you." He shuffled closer to her. "Even now that still is on my mind. Yet you are trying to help me. Why?"

"We are family and families help each other. All my life I have wanted to know about my birth family, my roots. You and I, we are related by blood."

"Do you really think Nicholas and Catherine will forgive me? I almost believe you. I—"

A rumble shook the ground. Nicola fell on her knees.

"My dear gel," Malcolm helped her to her feet. "We must hurry away. They are blowing the buildings down to make way for the new docks. I had forgotten." He grabbed hold of her arms pulled her back to the building.

The wall they stood beside started to sway at the top and roll downward. Nicola held her hands over her ears. She watched it slide in slow motion as her uncle pushed her back toward the opened door.

"I am so very sorry, dear gel," he shouted out.

Something hit hard, and she felt herself falling.

****

Clay leaped over the fallen bricks littering the floor. He rushed over and sat down on the cold, wet, ground next to Nicola. He gingerly cradled her head in his lap. Blood seeped through his fingers the moment he touched the back of her head, and he probed carefully until he located the wound.

"The uncle is dead, buried under the wall. It is the strangest thing. The wall only fell where he was standing." Barnaby stood next to Malcolm's outstretched arm.

"Malcolm saved her life. I saw him push her away." Clay caressed Nicola's face and she opened her eyes.

"Uncle? Where is my uncle?" The sound of Nicola's voice was... His silent prayers had been answered. She tried to sit up.

"Lie still. I want to see if the bleeding from the cut on your head has stopped."

"Oh, my darling Clay. Is it you? I saw you and then my uncle—where is he?" She winced.

"The wall crushed him." Clay grasped her hand. "He saved your life, but I'm afraid he is dead."

"I have to see if there is anything I can do."

It was pointless to try to keep her lying down, so Clay helped her up. Her legs were shaky. He kept his arm around her waist as they moved over to the fallen bricks. She reached down to Malcolm's hand to feel for a pulse and found none.

"We must get the bricks off him," she said through sobs. "I-I have to see him...I have to." She closed her eyes and sighed. "I cannot leave. I will not."

"We cannot stay here." Clay touched his head to her forehead.

"Miss Nicola, you be all right?" Eel appeared beside her.

Another blast shook the building. The rumble of bricks hitting the ground not far from where they stood rolled around them. The ground shook under their feet.

"Eel, what are you doing here?" She looked puzzled and concerned.

"Did not think you should be 'ere by yourself, not in the East End. So I come to find you. A friend told me where you be."

"Later, Eel. You must stop the blasting now," Clay said. "Where are your friends?"

The blasting could be heard in other buildings. The explosions appeared to be in some type of sequence. Soon a series of blasts would hit their location again.

Eel whistled, and in a matter of seconds, the area was filled with people of all ages. Clay explained what needed to be done, and a short time later, all blasting stopped. Runners appeared and took over the job of removing Malcolm's body.

Nicola stood and waited to see her uncle's body emerge from the rubble. As she was turning to leave, she reached down, picked up a silver and bone button lying next to him, and placed it in her pocket.

The collapsing wall had crushed his skull killing him instantly. Nicola started to sway. Clay scooped her up and carried her outside.

"I know, my dear. But this ending was better than hanging."

"You are right, but he was my uncle, however misguided he was."

"I am very sorry for all you have been through."

She buried her head against his shoulder.

He carried her until they found the carriage and Barnaby. The trip to Aunt Belle's home was done in record time.

"Nicola, please, I am begging you to listen to me

without interrupting," Clay said, after settling her down on her bed. He got down on one knee. "Will you marry me? I love you with all my heart and soul. I want to spend the rest of my life with you."

She scampered off the bed, dirt and all. "You still are the most—I haven't found a word to describe you yet, but I will. I love you, too, and wish to be with you forever."

They sealed their promise with a kiss, a very hot and delicious kiss.

Nicola looked up at Clay with half closed eyes. "The current between us is still there."

"It will be with us always, my love." Clay reached down for another promising kiss.

Epilogue

The announcement of the marriage of Catherine Highbridge and Nicholas Lynford, Duke of Russellton, the introduction of their grown daughter Nicola, and Malcolm's part in the Cato Conspiracy kept the gossip mill galloping wildly as it crisscrossed the entire country. There wasn't a town or a dwelling that missed the *Ton* gossip. It was decided in more than one drawing room that it was the scandal of the century.

Nicola and Clay chose to have a quiet family wedding with only their families present. They were wed on a warm, sunny day at Highbridge Manor. The sweet fragrance of roses mixed with carnations and lilies filled the air. A light breeze filtered through the open windows and caused the scent from the beautiful bouquets to mingle as the air current meandered through the room.

****

Six months later Nicola stood outside with the open door at her back, as she watched Clay ride down the driveway of their London home.

I still for the life of me do not understand my husband. He amazes me. I told him the wonderful news and he said, "Magnificent, my dear," and left for his afternoon ride to his club.

"Sister Dear, we need to talk to you," Mara said, as Emmy ran up to stand next to her.

Nicola walked back into the house, closing the door behind them. "Sister Dear means you two are up to something."

"You wound me, us." Emmy put her hand to her heart.

"Yes, well, every time you say 'Sister Dear' you want me to do something." Nicola stuck her chin in the air.

Both young women looped their arms through Nicola's and escorted her into the library.

"You are right. We are up to something." Mara sighed. You found your parents, and we want you to locate ours as well. We too, want to know our family's history."

"Do you think Catherine would provide any information to us?" Emmy asked.

"I cannot answer for my mother. You will have to ask her yourselves. I would be willing to assist you." Nicola chewed on her bottom lip "You both need to understand I will *help*—but not take over your pursuit of your birth parents."

"We do not know where to begin," Emmy said, fingering her necklace. "How about if we help you?"

Clay burst through the door. He threw his hat and coat on the floor.

"What did you say when I was leaving? I was preoccupied. I just realized that I heard you say—"

"We are going to have a babe in June." Nicola turned to her husband with a smug smile on her face.

He picked her up and twirled her around.

"Clay, you are making me dizzy. Please put me down."

"So does that mean you will not support us in our

search for our parents?" Emmy frowned at Mara.

"Yes, it is what this means," Clay said. "Nicola is not going to scour all over England looking for your parents. She needs to take care of herself and our child."

She gave him a sound kiss and a hug. Nicola then looked around his shoulder, thinking she'd distracted him. She winked at her sisters. After all, she was bound by her oath to The Sisterhood of the Coin.

Author's Note

The Cato Street Conspiracy

On February 23, 1820, the entire British Cabinet was scheduled to have a dinner at the home of Lord Harrowby in Grosvenor Square in London. The Spenceans, led by Arthur Thistlewood, an English revolutionary, planned to assassinate them, and intended to then form a provisional government.

The British authorities were aware of the Spenceans and Thistlewood's actions, but they were unable to pursue them without evidence showing their intent.

The government entered into an agreement with Edwards, a member of the Spenceans. He spied for the government. From testimony during the trial, it appeared he might have planned a great deal of the Cato Street Conspiracy.

Edwards was responsible for recruiting many men into the group and provided their weapons. He received no punishment for his part in the plot.

Richard Smithers, a Bow Street Runner, died at the hand of Arthur Thistlewood. His death was the only one reported from the actions at Cato Street.

Five men were hanged for high treason on May 1, 1820: Thistlewood, Ings, Burnt, Davidson described as a man of color, and Tidd. Other members were transported for life: Harrison, Wilson, Cooper, Strange, and Bradburn. The article in *The London Times* May 1, 1820, did not state where they were transported, but one would guess to Australia.

I added Malcolm Lynford into the conspiracy and he is a product of my imagination. I used the fictional

Charles Marker as an informant because my story required one.

A word from the author...

I grew up in Wisconsin and for many years lived in Northern California, where I received my MBA, raised my two children, and worked in the high tech industry based out of the Silicon Valley. My husband and I currently live in rural Kansas on an old farm homestead. Traveling and taking photographs go hand in hand, and I do both as much as I can. I love to read, so writing just seemed a natural progression.

http://www.zminor.com